MW00578463

ÆDNAN

LINNEA AXELSSON

ÆDNAN

AN EPIC

Translated from Swedish by Saskia Vogel

ALFRED A. KNOPF · NEW YORK · 2024

THIS IS A BORZOI BOOK PUBLISHED BY ALFRED A. KNOPF

English translation copyright © 2024 by Saskia Vogel

All rights reserved. Published in the United States by Alfred A. Knopf, a division of Penguin Random House LLC, New York, and distributed in Canada by Penguin Random House Canada Limited, Toronto. Originally published in Sweden as *Ædnan* by Albert Bonniers Förlag, Stockholm, in 2018. Copyright © 2018 by Linnea Axelsson. This translation published by arrangement with Bonnier Rights, Stockholm, Sweden.

www.aaknopf.com

Knopf, Borzoi Books, and the colophon are registered trademarks of Penguin Random House LLC.

Portions of this work originally appeared in *Orion*, *Agni* (Issue 94), *Freeman's: Animals* (October 11, 2022), *Words Without Borders* (March 2019), and *The Cortland Review* (Issue 87).

Library of Congress Cataloging-in-Publication Data

Names: Axelsson, Linnea, 1980– author. | Vogel, Saskia, translator.
Title: Ædnan : an epic / Linnea Axelsson ; translated from Swedish by Saskia Vogel.
Other titles: Ædnan. English
Description: First American edition. | New York : Alfred A. Knopf, 2024. | "This is a Borzoi book"
Identifiers: LCCN 2023001944 (print) | LCCN 2023001945 (ebook) | ISBN 9780593535455 (hardcover) | ISBN 9780593535462 (ebook)
Subjects: LCGFT: Domestic fiction. | Novels in verse.
Classification: LCC PT9877.1.X464 A4313 2024 (print) | LCC PT9877.1.X464 (ebook) | DDC 839.73/8—dc23/eng/20230519
LC record available at https://lccn.loc.gov/2023001944
LC ebook record available at https://lccn.loc.gov/2023001945

Jacket photograph by Julian Ward/Millennium Images, UK
Jacket design by Linda Huang

Manufactured in Canada
Published January 9, 2024
Reprinted One Time
Third Printing, November 2024

Of their
peculiar light
We keep one
ray
To clarify
the Sight
To seek them
by —

—EMILY DICKINSON

ÆDNAN

I

*Night camp at Lake Gobmejávri, near to where
Sweden, Finland, and Norway meet. Early spring 1913*

(BER-JONÁ)

The voice

the cup that memory
fills
I drink your hair
and soar

–

Through the fells
that birthed us and
twine us together

your body and mine

–

Fingers search
and the heart

howls

–

Here
where I wander

–

A rangeland runs
from the forest snow to
the windswept shore

–

There my herd scrapes
and leads us
land to land

prying me from
your arms

–

Alone
among the lichen

II

Two births. Two sons.

(BER-JONÁ)

A salty sea breeze
unfurled
your dark locks

We'd made it to our
summer grounds off the
north Norwegian coast

–

The cooling wind
ruffled
their strands of fur

Blew away
the midges
gave them no chance
to sting

–

The reindeer
lazily shook
its crown

–

happy at home
in the land of ease

–

The island's slope
a greening pillow
where the ocean soars

and the silver brooch
from the market square
was fixed to your shawl

–

In the calves' legs
the future twitched
uncertainly

in one direction
and in the other

–

Then the ocean depths
silently resettled
themselves:

painstakingly calm
and sly

–

On the move
to our winter grounds
across glowing
autumn pastures

you would birth
our sons

–

Two births
two sons

–

Aslat with his wreath of hair
black as soot
thick as a reindeer's coat

–

Honed fingers
that felt
the family mark

cut into the reindeer's ear

–

But that Nila

All he sensed
were the waves

–

Bluish black murky brown
Nila's eyes remained:

A newborn's veiled
deep listening gaze

–

Around that soul
a face was held

\-

Like a bowl

that never seemed
burdened by
or even aware of
its contents

\-

Large pieces
were carved
from our herd's
life cycle

Nila's weakness
gnawed me
down to the marrow

\-

Clawing feelings
took me
as their home:

Aversion
conceit
shame

\-

Ristin
you said the boy belonged
to a more sensitive kind

which had but assumed
human traits

And I saw something cunning
reveal itself

–

In his young mouth's
mysterious greetings
his irritating attempts
to reach out

–

No

–

You said his face
made it known that
much of him remained
in the oblivion
from which we all come

–

The ocean

quite simply
immeasurable

–

I gave my verdict:

You can't take
a weakling like that
into the fells

–

Someone like that is left
in our lodgings

or boards with the Swede
on his farms

–

Quarrel's sneer

was spread across
our faces

–

People stood back
silence lay in our hut

–

But that was before

Later you went around
with Nila roped to you
at the waist

–

Not one word would
pass the
weakling's lips

–

Too strong was
this mark
from behind
the water's veil

where mankind

–

spins its
origins

–

A tail fin or
a scut

that should have fallen off

–

He ought to have
swum out and returned
is what I said back then

–

Never will he
be of use

in the reindeer forest

III

Through the Rostočearru mountain pass. Spring 1913

(BER-JONÁ)

The expanses
their boundlessness

the reindeer herder cairns

–

Backs that burned
and feet

like bundles

–

Beating
our canes

to frighten
off the wolverine

–

On a sunny spring hill

rested our
pregnant does

–

We heard
heartbeats in the ground

Faint
beneath the inherited
migration paths

–

our son Aslat and I

–

Aslat would follow
the future's ground

–

It had not yet been
born into the world:

It would come
from the lives of our does

–

The wind had a long talk
with the tent's tarp

–

We look up
through the smoke hole
see the clouds

–

gliding by

–

A wide-awake doe
shakes her coat
until it whirls

Another stretches
her joints

–

They're grazing

So they will
stay calm for at least
another hour

–

Once they've woken up
properly

they'll keep
heading west

–

Into the mountains
to the calving grounds

–

Teeth mashing
milling their feed

The calves in wetness
treading

the heat
of the as-yet unborn

–

Our dark-headed son's
landscape

–

Ski stroke by ski stroke
song after song

we spread out the
landscape of our kin
in his body

–

Singing forth
the world around us

–

We sang the mountain
that looked like
an old woman

–

The hiding places
and fear
we sang

when the Swede
had gone to war

–

Against our
well-worn drum

–

The sky brightened

And we sang
father's father

–

sun
in hand

–

The hot
southern cliffs where
the spring bears
had their daytime dens

were sung forth

–

The meltwater

rippling
by the windbreak

–

Our son's light
singing voice

in which our kin's and
the land's memories
wished to fasten

–

Glided away

like the clouds toward you

Ristin

–

Trailing far behind

With the other families
headed for our spring camp

–

And the weak
boy

who had
to travel with you
and not us

–

His gaze like
the sea

which I had taught
myself to love

–

A cleansing bath
that gaze of his

–

We sang the work
and the reindeer

who led our family
apart

–

The reindeer who
taught us to use
the tundra

–

The sun stood silent
above steep cliffs

–

Quickly
Aslat and I
erected a small cairn

as a greeting
to those
behind us

–

Then all we had to do
was keep following
the reindeer colors

The wandering
herd:

like ocean waves

–

Brownish-gray back coat
white and downy
bluish white close
to the skin

–

black-tipped

–

The does streamed
gently up
the slope

–

The fact of breathing
ongoing

billows of reindeer colors

–

To be without
the reindeer's gaze
was impossible

–

The herd's body
became our bodies

our family

–

Only in the flow of work

was my longing absent

–

Then I only saw
antlers
possibilities
in the group

order

–

The dogs gave
bark and held
the herd together

–

The does' bells
clanged
against the scarp

They were used to
walking here and the work
was not hard

–

They were always drawn
westward
to give birth

in their special valley

–

And the sun left
our son's
thick crown

I watched it
shrivel like
dead twigs

–

Someone had to
climb up the cliff

to see if
we could take
our usual route

–

And his foot

sprang up

–

He slipped
and fell
from the rock

–

The ocean rises
the ocean gathers

Viscous waves
thick as marrow

–

Red trails of light
moved
before my eyes

until all went
dark and
veiled

–

His legs
black out

they drown
fading

–

The world was exchanged

–

And he came
up changed

–

On that cliff
Aslat's leg was crushed

IV

Meanwhile at Gobmejávri

(RISTIN)

That spring
my longing tasted
of rainwater

–

On a wing
we had ridden

made of the heat
of skin
and voice

–

On the reindeer's
shaggy branches

we were caught

–

There we were left hanging
driving in the wind

while the tundra of work
settled calmly
between us

–

The herd was what
nourished my blood
it fashioned me
with its world

–

The source
of my life's pattern

–

A rhythm of tasks

that were flayed and
cracked out of
the reindeer

–

Removing hair from hide
sewing the hide
making use of the meat

–

Carrying along
this animal-body
in remade parts:

Nourishment garments
products tools

–

In the evening
the stars flocked

–

They appeared and
mirrored themselves in the embers
in the middle of the tent

–

I snapped a
stick and fed
the flame

Brushed a piece
of straw off our
younger boy's arm

–

Then Nila's face
churned around its core

–

He shook
his head

eyes fixed tossing
his hair

–

He who could
also be so careful
and gentle

–

When he held
the sugar crate
the bentwood box

–

My friend beside me
sat spinning
with her daughters

–

Between their teeth
they pulled tendons
from the reindeers' legs

and twined them
into thread against their cheeks

–

The embers changed color

Ber-Joná they spun you
who were with the calving
does

–

They spun the sun above
the calving grounds
soothing

to the steaming new
bodies

–

Well-developed
fully evolved
calves

woven through
with heartbeats

–

A fresh continuance
of our life

–

As if of their own accord
Nila's fingers scratched
my back

while my friend
and I told
her girls:

–

Let the fire
keep you company

Remember that the people
you long for at work
far away

are looking up

–

at the same stars

–

Their tired eyes
are coming to rest
on the same fading embers

–

Our dark-haired
son's crown

–

When Aslat was born

I'd never seen
as dark

–

and thick a wreath of hair
as Aslat's

V

The accident site

(BER-JONÁ)

And Aslat
opened his eyes

and he screamed
out loud
and sobbed

–

I didn't know why

but I had
dragged him a ways
up the rock

–

And twilight
filled the valley

–

Darkness trickled
down the slopes
toward the plains

where the men
were running

in their soft
leather shoes

–

The wet snow
began to freeze

–

Someone said

that the unrest would cause
the does to panic

–

So they needed to be
set in motion

up the other
slope

–

My brother had been
standing on his own
awhile

–

I felt myself
tear up

When he came over
to talk to me:

–

We have to help
Aslat into
the food sled

–

We'll have to
transport him
that way

VI

The women break camp

(RISTIN)

Gingerly

I bound up
my memories

–

Treacherous company

coming and going
as they pleased

–

They rose up
and knocked me over

–

The snow crust gleamed
and I put
my pack on

–

Our weak boy
waited calmly

35

on his own skis

–

He too picked up
the backpack
of his heart

took care
when stacking
the wood

–

Perhaps

he did

–

The squeeze of my pack

reminded me of
when our boys
were small

–

We were still migrating
all together back then

hiking
in heavy rain

–

I hold the weakling
by the hand

For long stretches
Nila walks on his own

–

like his brother Aslat does

–

The water seeps
into Nila's clothes
which darken

and we battle
the wind to
raise our tent

–

Then we lie down
and wait out
the rain

–

The clothes are
hung to dry

–

And I wipe out
the coffee cups
with a rag

place them in
the large kisa

–

I touch the bag of flour
the silver brooch

–

One evening
Ber-Joná takes his time
waking up

The sun had been warming
the whole day through

–

And he is lying still

Letting his thoughts
grow clear

–

Aslat sits and
listens to the pack reindeer
grazing freely
near our camp

–

One is so tame
it sneaks up
to the tent

it nudges
the tarp

–

and Ber-Joná
mutters at it

Then he asks me
to mimic a grouse

–

Does this memory

gnaw at him too

–

Once

I tied Aslat
to a rock

–

I was working my way through
the cloudberry mire

–

I had such a heavy load
I took off my
bottoms

knotted my pant legs
and filled them with berries

–

The shawl and the smallest kerchief
that I could knot
the backpack

Full of berries

—

A black pool rose
through the moss

and the water was cold
pleasant on my neck

—

The golden eagle
dove darkly
from the sky

its eye yellow
and black

—

In that yellow eye

the world was
reflected differently

—

It reached out its claws
and sailed toward Aslat

I dropped the berries
and ran screaming
arms raised

—

Watched the heavy
bird of prey rise up and off

–

Everything was as usual

but this cast a shadow

–

And Nila he

–

was born dingy white

–

Face like a rag

this cast a shadow

–

My friend had placed
that slight figure
on my chest

–

She stretched out
his tiny limbs
and filled his palms
with her thumbs

But he would not grab hold

–

He lay still

arms outstretched

–

I saw his tender
heart flicker
under the skin

I saw the shadows
and that fine
rib cage

–

All the shadows
grabbing at
his chest

in an indifferent game

–

All those yielding
soft parts I saw

all that gave
way in him

–

All that

as soon as
he'd arrived
betrayed him

–

I said:

Take him out
into the air
we must rouse
his ire

–

The cold usually riles
them up

–

So my friend lifted
Nila out of the sugar crate

–

His fragile head
just drooped

Legs dangling slack
and head lolling
in her arms

when she stumbled
in the snow

–

Then I lay there a long while
looking at him

–

The waves sank
and surged again

that broad forehead
those wide-set eyes

–

My own features
rising rising

and Mama's features

–

By cheekbone
and eyebrow

–

I could sense that I was smiling

–

Perhaps I had
always been searching for
traces of Mama

outside of myself

VII

Through the Rosta River Valley from
Lake Ádjávárddojávrrit. Past the rivers
Tamok and Dápmoteatnu. 1913

(BER-JONÁ)

My brother and I
Aslat
we sang nothing

we no longer sang forth
the earth and
the memories

–

Vessels of song
formed by the voice

When words were not enough
for the lives
we lived

–

They had
trudged through hate

–

They had waded in sorrow

45

–

But through this deep-freeze
they could not come

we sang nothing

–

We simply watched as the fells
and the old migration routes
withdrew

from Aslat's body

–

From he who cannot

–

The flowing belt of reindeer
wandered keenly
along the cliffs

–

To feel their breath

to be left to dissolve with the sea

–

We moved slowly on
after several daylong
breaks

–

Once May Day passed

we were allowed to cross
the border into Norway

–

There was ever more bare earth

and the pregnant
does swayed on
in a dense pack

–

With a few
single calves
born
along the way

–

An impatient courage
had come
over the animals

who wanted most of all
to break into a trot

–

Our son's dog ran
barking along
the edges of the herd

Both our dogs
had to obey
my hand now

–

And the does
calved

–

One calf wouldn't
come and we had to
pull it out

It was
so stuck
dead

–

it was large

–

Many were calmed
by the sight of others
birthing nearby

but some
withdrew
and wanted to be
alone

–

We sang nothing

–

A reigning
silence

from Aslat's seat
in the food sled

–

In the legs
and abdomen:

an unshakable
baggage

–

Evening came

And I fed
him a big pot
of reindeer broth

–

With each spoonful
he disappeared deeper
into this new

silence

–

And I let him
take out his sorrow
on my arms

my chest

VIII

Along the Könkämä River. Spring camp at Suvigorsa. 1913

(RISTIN)

My friend's daughters
skied in line
in front of me

And the wind
braided their
scattered voices

–

They were wondering
how it was going for
the does

–

Those girls who always
helped me with
Nila and
raising the tent

warmed me
when I was cold

–

The moonlight coursed
over our pack reindeers'
long backs

gray and silky
the animal gaze moved
over the snow crust

–

And their grunts
rose up

from their cleft hooves
a crackling rose
in waves

–

And the fell's crown
darkened

–

Right across the Swedish border

on the Finnish side
I knew that there was
a church

–

Along this valley
the does would
wander toward Norway

our does and Aslat

\-

A shivering child was in tears
and I pointed
to the shore

on the far side of the lake

\-

I told the child about the silver
that my father
had buried there

black patches
on the mountain's
southern slopes

\-

The temperature rose

and the air and sounds
felt more alive
as other migrating groups
drew near

\-

We lay in the spring camp
waiting for
the spring flood
to flow by

\-

We did not plan on
moving until June

—

I braided my hair in the sun

Listening to an old
woman who said she didn't
have it in her to hike to her
summer slope in Norway this year

—

The palm of her
aged face cracked
fumbled for support

one-armed

—

Second week of May

and many had already
entered Norway

—

The young people longed

They filled the whole camp
with their longing

—

They wanted to go to the sea

to the market
on the square

–

One night

we awoke
to distant barking
and shouts

–

The barking of dogs echoed
between the fells and woke
the whole camp

Most of us got up
and spied toward
the slope

–

At the farthest end
of the valley's mouth
a gray-brown streak

–

was flowing along
the side of the fell

–

The dogs were
but dark spots
gliding around

but the reindeer herders
with their tired bodies
were radiant

–

There appeared to be
bulls among the does
and calves

No

–

This was not you
and our Aslat

coming
through the valley

IX

The summer camp on the island of Kvaløya, Norway.
Summer 1913

(RISTIN)

Do not come here

Do not come near
my boys

–

How silently you neighbors
streamed in along
the slopes

with your does and
lovely calves

–

While the kolt on
Aslat's emaciated
body just flapped
in the wind

Like a sail
slapping his back

–

not carrying him
anywhere

–

Stay away from us

–

I will stand guard
like the eagle
washed up
on the beach

where the sea
spit us out

–

Like the seagull
I will dive after
fish for them

–

Like the bear
I will rest with
my boys

–

The lapping of waves on the shore
is so pleasant

between the rocks
the good berries hide

–

A simple home
glitters at the water's edge

A nursing home
where I will care for those
with whom I want to be

–

And for us it cannot
be warm enough
or soft enough

at home in the eagle's nest

–

You who force your way
in with weepy eyes

and those faces
on which your mouths
are smeared:

–

Go away

do not wail for us

–

I will sniff out
a new world and draw up
to the burrows of the weak

here they shall want
for nothing

–

You shall make offerings
of meat and silver

Carry them
to the shore and
go your way

–

I will never leave them

–

I bring my boys
close to my heart

I intend to carry them
because I can

–

And when I falter

I will hold on
to my pipe

–

I can smoke my pipe

and feel its familiar
shape in my hand
between my lips

–

I can sit with the fire

let the fire warm
my solid armor

–

Steel I sew into
my silken shawl and
my chest becomes a shield

so no one will see
this racing heart

–

This pecking bird
alone and small

Enveloped by
a great
patient nurse

–

Soon they will awaken
my sad boys

–

One boy sadder
than the other

each night even angrier

–

Never again shall this family
long on split paths

where the sea
folded in shadows

–

You cannot make us
go again

–

Never again will I spread
out the mantle of our home

as we follow
the herd

X

(ASLAT THE DEAD)

You left me
on the Swede's farm

alone and wrapped
in my large kolt

–

I did not stay there

–

One fall and one winter
we cried together

Then you rejoined
the herd and
drew away

–

As for me I spread
my kolt into wings
and set my course

emptied my body
of blood and
vanished

–

I could not stay

Where I had fallen and
was never to rise
again

–

Could you feel it Papa

me blowing across the sea

–

Didn't you hear me

Among the seabirds
as you came walking
with your summer-fat
reindeer

–

I was the lone
strand from the reindeer's coat
gliding across the sea

in the bay by
the reindeer's swimming spot

–

And the fine hill
in the late summer sun

Where the herd
had to find its own way
down the cliffs

–

Until the thick fog rolled in

And it became
impossible to see
the pitch of the slope

–

I was the forest
thickening

around the great
forest path
that had been hewn
in olden times

–

Where your lead reindeer
scrubbed its antlers

–

Did you feel it Mama
in your hand

all the while you
milked that tame reindeer
who then disappeared
among the trees

–

To search for lichen
and mushrooms and lick
urine from the ground

–

I was the weight
in the stone you brought
back from the coast

to place on
my grave

–

One stone each summer

you carry home
to the winter grounds
Nila and you

–

Mama you caress
that scar on my
brother's forehead
as if it were a
whisper from me

–

Because I once
threw a wooden log
at him

that hit right there

–

Nila after my fall

–

You treated me
the same as you
always had

as though I
hadn't changed

–

The same
slow smile
while your head quietly
wanted to roll back
into place

deep between your shoulders

–

Nila did you feel it
I was the movement
under the boat

in the mountain lake where
Mama and you
spread the nets

–

Did you catch
my gaze
in the eye of the loon

–

I stood on a twig
my legs like
sticks

When the wind bent
back the yellowing
leaves

–

I saw unknown fells

with roaring rivers

–

And I flew above
the boat calling
to you all:

–

There will be rain
there will be rain

XI

Lake Dápmotjávri. Aslat's grave. Karesuando churchyard,
Norrbotten County. Late fall 1920

(BER-JONÁ)

That fall
the Lapp Administration
arrived

–

The ruling language
drizzled over us

Swedish words
impossible to pronounce

–

They penetrated
our clothes
coated our skin

–

That needling eye

–

a rain through
all that one loves

—

Dirty were we
living with dogs

semi-nomads who
followed cattle around

—

Women who
baked bread so tough
your teeth fell out

—

In the midst of the breeding ground
the Swede appeared
with the gathering storm

—

To hold forth
among our
does in heat

—

He bore a message
from the three
countries' men:

Swedes Norwegians
and Finns

—

Far from
the reindeer's world
several families
had been selected

We now had to force
our herds to graze on
unfamiliar grounds

–

We were to be driven
from the forests fells
and lakes

Migration paths and songs
had to be stifled
stricken from memory

–

The memory of the herd

the calves' legs
that had always
guided us home

–

Now they would be born
on other land

–

Now each step
homeward in autumn
was a departure from
our lives

–

My brother and the rest
said farewell to the trails
and hillsides

–

Never more would
we sit on the island's
sloping summer grounds
where the ocean smoothed
the stones

and where Aslat once
learned to walk

–

Then my stomach tied itself
into dark knots

–

While winter
as ever
whitened on

–

And we tried
to scare off wolves
we sped through frozen woods
to our winter home

–

There I watched the dusk
dwindle gray between
gray farms

–

In the birch forest
across the ice
was a group of tents

With pillars of smoke
rising beyond
the churchyard
where you were waiting
Ristin

–

Outside
the churchyard walls

by Aslat's grave

–

I took your hand

you had an
infected wound above
your eyebrow

–

You placed
the last stone
from the coast

on his grave

–

I had to hold
Nila's fingers
like jerking
reins

–

And the familiar
waves spoke
to me

of a freedom
in the sea

–

I said that I
hated the reindeer

but needed them
all the same

–

We have to leave
Aslat again

For work's sake
and the herd's

–

Here he would be left behind
all alone

While we were being driven
from our home

–

You said:

What kind of home is it
where no one dares say
our son's name

–

Aslat is forgotten

His fate is all
they remember

–

But you promised me

that his head was safe
at rest in his grave

–

The dead after all
were not allowed
to be exhumed

–

And the bells
tolled beyond
the forest

–

We were called
to a church weekend

–

This one last time
we would
be among our own

–

For now it was full

It was full of
people in the village

XII

Karesuando parish. Winter 1920

(RISTIN)

The Swede's fingers
filled my mouth

clothing strewn
across the floor

–

Me thinking
it was because of my
bad teeth

that the traveling doctor
had come

–

With hard tools
he measured me

literate men
in every nook

–

With scratching pens

they went
through me

–

I could tell that a
stocky figure
was taking shape
in their papers

In royal ink
that racial animal
was drawn

–

The shackles
of our obedience

–

unfastened
my home-sewn belt

–

My breasts sagged
their distaste blazed

–

I saw how they
wrinkled their
slender noses

laughing
all the while

–

My friend beside me
quickly helped
me on with my kolt

–

Then she whispered translations
of their questions
about how we handled
our menses

–

Over the doctor's shoulder
the church minister

–

I heard him
say in Finnish:

The way their men drink
makes God cry
and the Devil laugh

And the shame

–

took root in me

because of my dark hair
and my
dark eyes

–

Outside the barn
my friend's daughters
waited shivering
for their
treatment

–

And my poor Nila
was fished out

from where I do not know

–

A camera was pointed
at his
upset face

until he just
filtered through the floor

–

I watched them
trample him
with heavy boots

Tall chairs
were dragged out and they
took a seat on him

–

I noticed how big
he had gotten
not a child anymore

–

there he stood lost
and mute among their
bare hands
touching him

–

He should come
with us to the institute
the doctor said

and finally
my body obeyed

–

And I went up
to the men
and pulled the weakling
from the Swede's grip

XIII

The journey south. Early spring 1921

(RISTIN, BER-JONÁ)

Then we sat at length
in gloom

my friend and I

–

It was the sunless
time of year

when the light and the plants
gathered strength
underground

–

And the world
would be born anew

–

Knots of life
searching unseen
in the does'
inky stomachs

–

Untrodden paths
bided hidden

under hibernation's
shielding muffling
heavy suspense

–

You never knew which
circumstances were taking shape
in the night of winter

which grazing conditions
would emerge from the thaw

–

When the Lapp
Administration
took me

we were sitting around the fire

–

I was patching
something up

My friend's daughters
were mending a tear
in a large fur

when they arrived

–

when they came to take us
away

–

I packed carefully
taking in everything
that was unnecessary

and had to be left behind

–

I was already wearing
Mama's silver braid
on my back

–

Tired and
verging on old
I was reflected in my
friend's face

when we said farewell

–

Until the guides
interrupted us

without a word

–

With only looks
and silence

–

I followed them
into thawing
deep forests

–

The path was neither
snow nor earth
the ground moved
beneath me

–

The fellside slant

evaded me

–

Holes widened
in the ground

and I resisted
with my poles

–

While the guides
mounted guard
of their silence

–

They refused to reveal
to us the way

–

Even as Nila
was whipping his arms
so unsettled

I had to
drag him along
on a sled

–

There he lay
strapped tight and staring
as though he were being drowned
by all the new

–

Ber-Joná was following
the herd somewhere
far ahead

I could hardly
sing us anymore

–

After all I didn't know
what the ground was like
across which he was moving

And I wondered
if it was hard

–

Ristin
It was hard

our reindeer
didn't want to go south

–

They wanted to follow their
usual path

and the herd
was hard work

–

Only the dogs'
untiring work
spurred them on

–

One night we passed
the city of Kiruna

–

I saw the mighty
bright place
with its many lamps

And I sensed a
wave of fear
from Nila with you

–

as though caught in a storm

–

Someone said
we must almost
be there

–

An exhilarated
fatigue swept
through the men

And we were all
sleepy like small children

–

But it was a long way yet
to the river valley

XIV

The Great Lule River Valley. Spring 1945

(RISTIN, BER-JONÁ)

Long forest rivers
their mouths at the coast
rushing icy through the land

–

Iron-bearing regions
sparsely populated
wood- and moorland

–

Inexhaustibly the
currents flowed
from wellsprings
in the fells

and fell roaring
from escarpments

–

Farther down
the river channels quieted

–

Chains of lakes
muffled the water

and the stretches of
fishing waters
farmland
overtook

–

Then the yielding
moorland belt
met the currents

which strained

–

through the moss

–

The soft permeable
marshlands that let
the rivers swell into
wide gliding lakes

on their way
to the coast

–

Where they would scatter
with the waves

dissolve in the sea

–

But the Swede
was roving

he'd caught
the scent of game

—

Wild rivers
rushing untouched
in their deep grooves

And strong men
were sent up through
the forests

—

They were to tame
the river and yoke
the power of the rapids

—

Even though our kinsmen
had long moved with
their herds across
this rolling river valley

—

Fine winter roads
the river gave them when
it froze to ice

—

Their songs and
memories could be
cast

From the knickpoint's
foaming white
wild forms

–

But the Swede he dammed

And the river was left
muffled and silent
behind the dams' dim
stony blind walls

–

Shrouded the currents slid
down among turbine halls
deep below the fells

and flowed up
in places unforeseen

–

Bit by bit the herds
had to give way

–

And there I came
with our Nila

–

A rocky riverbank
we were allotted

A sheer drop into the deep
was the slope of that hill

–

And the eyes of our kinsmen

turned to us:

–

Go home
there's no room for you here

–

Your men don't keep
the herd together like ours do

Your reindeer are grazing our pastures
they're laying to waste
our forefathers' paths

–

During the day
our feelings shied
from the fight

evening
licked our wounds

–

All the while
the Swede was damming

–

and the water climbed
the hills

–

Town after town
the Swede erected
around his structures

–

With streets of iron
buildings of stone

Vast weighty
hard structures

–

Swedish women
arrived
to buy
from me

–

things I had crafted
of hide and horn

–

There I sat by the fire
crafting

while their men
dammed

–

Until the hill assigned to us
to build our hut
was drowned again

–

Twice Nila and I had to
tear down the peat hut I'd built
and move it higher
up the slope

–

Then we lay still
and listened

to the tortured
river's silence

–

I felt Nila
writhing
in our narrow bed

like a fish
flung onto land

–

He stormed
and scratched

until it tore
at my mother-heart

–

No we didn't belong to
those who still remembered
this river's
voice in song

when it had flowed freely

–

Out in the fells
Ristin

the herd skidded
across the ices

–

We had taken a new route

across the great
frozen mountain lake

–

A few reindeer herders we met
the kind who'd been migrating here
since olden times

had said the ice would hold

–

The ice creaked beneath
the herd which lowed
and ran and
skidded on their hooves

–

I thought I saw Aslat's old
dog sitting there
waiting in the dark
on the other side of the lake

in utter silence

–

as though it could sense
everything

–

That's when I heard the sound
of ice breaking

–

I saw waves rising
and recharging

–

At the same time I could see
with my own eyes

that the whole herd
had in fact made it safely to
the other side

–

And continued on
through the snow

–

Ber-Joná
what you heard
it wasn't the ice breaking

it was me

–

When a doctor arrived
from a hospital
on the coast

–

Who promised Nila
a bed of his own

and walks
along the beach

XV

An apartment on Postgatan, Porjus, Norrbotten County. 1946

(RISTIN)

Outside the window
the lamplight
glares

–

Strange star
never rests

shines all summer long

–

Fixed to the same
cables that lift
the river's
currents into the air

and lead them
far from here

–

Dear friend back on our
old summer island

Are there lamps
on the square now too

—

Do you meet the same
white chilly light

where you are

—

The curtain folds
become the grooved cliffs
across which we would wander
when I shut my eyes

and push out
the boat of the kitchen sofa

—

in my drowned realm

—

There bobs our son's
withered crown

—

I gather up all
the ocean-smoothed
stones

that we carried
to his grave

—

They float along the
wall that
the Norwegian raised

–

When he shut
his borders to us

–

And the Finn shut them
from the other end

so we were pushed down

–

To this apartment
by the dam

–

To the east
our overgrown boy gurgles

in his hospital
by the sea

–

Not the wide
summer sea
in Norway

But a shallow
inland sea

–

That almost freezes
to the bottom
in winter

in its innermost coves

–

Where the water is sweeter

from the catchment of
the forest rivers

–

By the tussock
I climb out of the boat:

Two birch trees
the sons we failed

–

Icebound
in each their age

–

Ber-Joná
Only you and I
grow older

–

The leaves of our faces

that fell from them

–

And the words we spoke
gusts of wind that
sometimes meet

–

There's stomping in the front hall

I sit up

–

Ber-Joná comes in
with a relative
from back then

Who still moves
in our old parts

–

He takes a seat
beside me
with his backpack
on his lap

then he takes out
a large book

–

With a wide

glossy cover

–

It's about us

That Swedish
traveling doctor
wrote it

–

He says:

I've got something to show you

–

He opens the book
to the photo
they took on that day

it's a picture
of our Nila

–

Ber-Joná runs
his finger
along the caption

and our relative
spells out for us
what they wrote:

–

Feeble-minded man

XVI

The sea exists

it breathed
beyond the corridors
the stairwells

–

Once
Eden's apple tree
bore fruit

and the buds on the large
lindens in the castle yard
were bursting

–

A lone nurse
makes her way
through the hospital

–

She passes the chapel

in the cafeteria
lingers the smell of dill

–

They had bathed

–

She'd sat
by the tub
kneading
his aching shoulders

–

She squeezes her
hands and smiles
to herself

–

They had practiced
how to speak

He was taught to
use a Swedish name

Nils

–

And no one
not even the head physician

could ever
take this away from her

–

Out in the park

bird cherry seeds rained
on the gravel paths

The seabirds shrieked

–

The waves turned
and again laid themselves
upon each other

Ædno

I

The same apartment on Postgatan, Porjus. Winter 1977

(LISE)

The waves

out there
they turn

–

Fumbling at
the dam's
back

–

Almost all of
my life I have followed
those waves

Seen the river come
running between
the fellsides

–

But here right
outside the brakes
are put on

it is held back

–

I can see that the river
wants to rush by

but the dam
is standing in its way

–

like an inhibition
out in nature

–

I have probably
always had a hard time
separating nature

from myself

II

Later that same night

(LISE)

The telephone rang

half asleep
I thought it was Per
crying again

–

Rolf sat up
wide awake

and I remembered
that he was on call

–

He went to
the telephone
and I heard
him speaking

–

Where would Rolf
be going tonight:

–

Seitevare Randi Ritsem
Messaure Ligga
Harsprånget Akkats

–

All these power plants

impossible to separate
from the lunch boxes made of
stainless steel that I
sent with him

filled with dinner leftovers

–

But also specially
made meals

–

The dog jumped
bright-eyed around
us in the kitchen

claws
clacking
on the floor

–

Then she stood awhile
on the plastic mat
and had a drink

While we waited
in silence at the kitchen table

–

A lone car
drove by

but it was
not his ride

–

I took out
a tray of food
from the freezer

–

Rolf's wash bag

from the cabinet in
the bathroom

–

The small leather pouch
with a drawstring that Mama
had once sewn

as a gift to him

–

She had given
it to Rolf
right as she
was about to leave

As part of
her bid to
get out of here

–

Surely to
avoid
his thanks

–

And his admiration

of her handiwork

–

I've never been
that good
with my hands

–

From inside the room
I heard our daughter
whimper

–

Rolf
I didn't want
Sandra to get up

to yet again

–

plant herself like a
tiny watchman between
you and me

–

The murk
in my chest pressed
into my throat

And the car came
to a stop
down on the street

–

I went back
to bed

without a word

–

Relieved that I
couldn't think of
anything to say

that neither of us
had started
anything

–

Sandra and Per
were breathing easy
on Rolf's side
of the bed

–

Meanwhile his blanket
and pillows
were cooling on the sofa

where he'd been sleeping
since Per was born

–

Half a year ago

after having hung
in the air for so long

–

Because Rolf
and I noticed

that we needed to
surround ourselves with
one more child

–

At dawn

the phone rang again

–

I got up to
answer it but
no one was there

–

Only that mournful
gaze that watched
me sometimes

from inside the kitchen

–

The dead old
woman's gaze

Ristin

–

The woman who'd had
this apartment
before us

Nila's mother

–

Nila who charged
around on the slopes
back home in Änonjalme

and who Mama
had talked about
so often

–

The overgrown
boy

–

Who frightened off
Mama and the other children
with his cries when he
hit his mother

and who'd simply come
walking one day

–

Together with the
tightly forged group
of young women who had been
forcibly removed here

–

I can still tell
by their grandchildren's
and great-grandchildren's
caps

–

In church and at
graduations

who comes
from Karesuando

–

Their caps aren't
like ours

–

Now there she was again
lying on my kitchen sofa
wearing that lace-trimmed cap

As if embalmed
in a sarcophagus

–

A boat drifting
around on a dead sea
that was there just
for her

that was rocking her

–

What load
had she carried
bursting
behind her forehead

squirming
on the inside
of her cheeks

–

I stood there
receiver in hand

Taking in her slender
fingers at rest
on her womb

And I thought that everything

–

had yet to slip
from my hands

–

But I was so
angry at Rolf

I thought I
might grind
my teeth to bits

–

And really I couldn't
stand

Anyone
but the children
looking at me

III

Änonjalme. 1956

(LISE)

I ran across
the rocks

along the way I broke
off a stick
for waving

–

My feet knew
the lay of the boulders
and I flew across
the rocky shore

–

The rugged
beach of
blasted rock

–

Scraped up

from some dam site
and spread along
our side of the river

125

–

Behind me I heard
my brother who
was throwing a stone
into the water

Jon-Henrik called out:
Lise
dála Áhttje boahtá

–

And I looked
around

–

High above the cabin

I caught sight of Papa
limping silently
down the hillside

–

A few snared
grouse dangling slack
from his shoulder

and I rushed
onward

–

The river respired
at rest in the sun

–

The yellow leaves had
begun to dry out

–

The thickets thinned

and the cliffs
scattered the trails
underfoot

–

I sank down
in my usual
spot

at the edge of
the slope

–

The mountain folded
itself into a deep
bench

close to the river which
flowed past

–

With my back
to the cliff

I studied
the fells
before me

on the other side
of the river

–

My eyes followed
a familiar path across
the cliffs' unmoving broad
blind faces

Which had always seen me
had answered me
kept me company

–

For as far back as I
could remember

–

The snow-clad domes

and the mountainsides
streaked with ice that
seemed to be so near

–

As if I only
needed to reach out
my hand to
touch them

Though it would
take several days
on foot to get there

–

And I sensed
how the currents
were gently sweeping
me off

all the way to the sea

–

Where the river would
dissolve in
the waves

–

Far out in the Gulf of Bothnia

and mix with
the other rivers

–

Julevätno mixed
with Gájnajädno
Vuojatätno and
the Pite River

perhaps there were
even more rivers

–

Even more waters
and winter roads made of ice

along which our dialects had
been carried then spread
across the earth

–

Until Vattenfall arrived

dammed up the old
sea routes and redirected
the rivers

–

Opened the taps of their
great flooding
reservoirs and
made new lakes

so the river had
to find its way forward

–

Through discharge tunnels

sector gates

–

These foreign words

that come from
the spread Mama
can rustle up

–

When someone from
Vattenfall stops by
for a coffee

In exchange for
a bit of news from
downstream

–

I had to pee and
stood up

pulled down my pants

–

The urine ran hot
along the cool
yellowish

rusty gray-speckled
steplike boulders

–

When I ran
back later

my panties
were still damp

–

Lise

Mama shouted
from the boat

–

And life cut in

it wrapped itself
around my neck

–

When I heard
my new name

–

My name had
been Susanna

until this spring
I had been Susanna

–

Then I came down with a fever

–

and Grandpa Lise
had appeared to
Mama in a dream

To get her to
name me after
him instead

—

The boat came in

And my tongue
was lost amid those
many big tangled
wet nets

and Mama's
great silent
closed face

—

As usual
she tells stories as
we empty the nets

one about a woman
who had a boat

—

She tore apart the boat
and built a smoker

tore apart the smoker and
built a bench
tore apart the bench and
built a stool

—

Then she tore apart the stool

—

And then
she had nothing
left

and with that the whole
net was empty

–

Go on clean the fish
Mama said

–

And I let
my fingers listen
their way forward

While the stones
on my tongue
slowly dissolved

–

Hey Mama
I said

how come your dad
was called Lise

–

And she said
haven't you already
heard that one

–

But I asked again
why was Grandpa
given a girl's name

–

Well it's because his name
was Elias

–

He was supposed to be called Elias

–

When the priest
came to our hut for
the catechetical meeting

his first question was
if there were any
new children

–

They said yes

his name is Elias

–

But when
the priest returned
the following spring

–

he asked how it
was going with little Lisa

–

No one
dared tell
the priest that he'd
heard wrong

so instead they start
calling your grandpa
Lisa

–

Or Lise

as he would
say

–

But let's rinse
the fish now
Mama said

–

In the distance

at the other end of
the beach

I saw Jon-Henrik
come walking
toward us

—

The magazine
shoved into
his waistband

—

A comic book
he'd been given last
summer

when some people from
Vattenfall passed
by ours

—

They didn't
have anything
for me

They'd just
pinched my
cheek

—

That night my brother lies
beside me for a long time
on the pull-out sofa

flipping through
that comic

—

137

It's hot
under the blanket

It's one of the
blankets that Papa had
taken from the Swedish
Tourist Association

–

Papa's job had been to walk
through the mountains
from cabin to cabin

–

And swap out the
ragged blankets
for the new ones he
had with him

–

Now and then

Jon-Henrik's
small slender feet nudge
my fingers

–

Is it just me
who's wondering if
we're friends

–

I'm half asleep

when in the light
of the fire I see
the shadow

–

draped
across the chair

–

Someone
has laid out
Jon-Henrik's kolt

IV

The next morning

(LISE)

The yellow light
reaches me through
the window

warms me
in the morning
wakes me slowly

–

Jon-Henrik's
eyes are still shut
in the darkness at
my feet

–

He never wants
to sleep with his face
in this direction

where the sun comes in

–

The autumn light is so golden
it spreads between
the soft leaves

comes out of
the cloudberry jam

–

That Mama
sets out

I can't wait

–

Cloudberry jam
with milk
for us to eat

–

Cloudberry jam just for us

–

I wake Jon-Henrik

he can't wait
to have some
either

–

The flame-orange
cloudberries soothe
like smooth sap

While the kolt
over on the chair
stares blue

swallows the light

–

The bland white
coffee cheese squeaks
between my teeth

and crumbles
in my mouth
as I chew

–

Papa has already
gone out

–

And I ask
Mama why
Jon-Henrik's kolt
is hanging there

–

He's going to put it on
she says

the boat he's
hitching a ride on
will probably be here soon

–

You're starting school today
she says loudly to
Jon-Henrik

143

not looking
at either of us

–

And it's
strange but

–

my feet no longer
reach the floor

–

Slowly I crush
a cloudberry seed
between my teeth

I see that
Jon-Henrik
has started to cry

–

I ask:

Which school

–

And Mama says
that he'll be
moving to Porjus

–

Where he will live
with another family

but will be
back home for
Christmas

–

There's a knock on the door
and a few Swedes
come in

I've never
seen them before

but Papa

–

comes in after them

–

Mama takes Jonne's
clothes off and
dresses him in the kolt

–

She pulls the
studded belt
tight around his waist

as if around a large
limp doll
with no strength

–

And no
way out

–

Except the Swedes' boat

lying there
unlit and in wait down
by the beach

–

And that I never
even saw come
sailing

–

I suspected nothing

I didn't know
that this was going
to happen

–

Jonne did you know

–

Did Papa tell
you

that he would put
his hand on your back

and shove you toward
that boat

—

And why
didn't you say anything
to me

V

The apartment in Porjus. Winter 2013

(LISE)

Mama what are you
keeping quiet about

Sandra asked
yesterday

–

As if she were
fully aware of
the load that
she'd been given

and maybe
she is aware

–

Sandra who has
gone and married a
reindeer keeper now

–

And fights for
every Sámi
question

as she puts it

–

I shake out
another cigarette

–

Smoke gently
under the fan

fondling the smoke

–

Remembering Grandmother's
gesture when she stuffed
her pipe

–

I can hear
Rolf walking
into the hall

as if it
were yesterday

–

And the children
unzipping
their overalls

–

I see Sandra

sitting at the table
fifteen years old

–

We're eating

–

And she puts
down her fork and says:

–

Tell me what it
was like at the Nomad School
Mama

I'm supposed to write
an essay about
you in school

–

And I did not

want to talk about it

–

Not all of a sudden

–

With Rolf listening
and Per looking at me
with curiosity

–

The latticework of silence
its familiar crackling around
the soft heart

–

But it will be spring

somewhere the bluethroat
awakens sings

–

Inside me
something opens loosens
lets in the years

–

I stub out my cigarette

and go over
to the dresser

–

Sit down on the floor
and pull out the
bottom drawer

–

One by one

I take out
the old caps
I've been saving

–

The ones I've turned
inside out

–

Until one of the children
comes along and wants
to use them

–

I turn Aunt
Ella's cap
Aunt Susanna's cap
right side out

and then Grandma
Máret's cap

–

The red one
with forest-green
trim

that she wore
so often

–

This was the cap
Sandra had worn

when the police put
their hands on
her head

–

And pushed
her to the earth

–

This earth
that she loves so much

earth that she and her
friends want to protect
from overseas
mining concerns

–

The police
tore this cap
right off
Sandra's head

Now this memory can no
longer be separated

from Grandma's cap

–

Which I must have
seen her wear
a hundred times

when she rowed out
across the water

–

What if I had done
more than just listen

–

When Aunt Ella
talked about the Lapp
as a primitive
human

who knew
nothing of the
great big world

–

What if I had instead
asked her

why she'd say a thing like that

–

Deeper down in the drawer

lay Mama's piles
of colorful shoe bands
which I've saved

–

Bands she wrapped
around pieces of
cardboard she cut

from the phone book
cover

–

I can tell at once
by how the bands are
wound and
how the lace
is folded

that this is
her work

–

I've uncovered so much
of what she
left behind

but never put it to use

–

Trimming ribbon and ruffles
torn loose
from other clothes

surely things
that were threadbare

–

Her many
buttons and
old needle books

–

The little needlecase
made of reindeer horn that she
had on her belt
that one time

–

The seaplane made
an emergency landing in the fells
and she was there

and had to mend
a tear in the wing
with sinew thread

–

You didn't usually
have the needlecase
on you Mama

But that time
you did

–

You who always said
that you were sure
I'd marry a Swede

because I was too
impractical for
Sámi life

–

Even though it was me
who stripped and
sanded this dresser
for you

–

Your wine-red tall
heavy dresser

That has become almost
like the dam out there

–

An embankment
where all that has
come to pass collects

in a gliding
great cold whirlpool
that mixes
up all of time

–

Leaches the color from
every emotion

–

I'm about to
open another drawer
when my phone
rings

Could be Sandra
maybe Per

–

But I don't make it
up and off the floor

in time to answer

VI

It's been a long
time since I heard you
this clear

and somehow alive
to the world as
yesterday Sandra

when you called

–

You said the verdict
had been passed

–

Girjas Sámi village
who is suing
the Swedish State

For hunting and
fishing rights within the
Sámi community's boundaries

–

You said:

Girjas won Mama
we won in Gällivare
District Court

–

Now we wait
for the State
to appeal

–

I needed
a long smoke

after we'd hung
up the phone

–

Will a new
trust in the State
now begin to grow

–

Or will the great Swede
put on ever weightier
armor

until we end up
in full-scale battle

–

What will you do then Sandra
which pathways do you
foresee in your struggle

above and beyond your voice

–

How many times now

haven't you asked
me to talk

–

Talk to me about your
life Mama
you say

without understanding
how embarrassed I get
when you say:

–

You have to write
your story down
Mama

write your history

–

talk about your journey

–

I haven't
been able to explain
to you Sandra how
wrong it feels

–

When you call
the fact that I
have existed and
am still here

my journey

VII

Låddejåkkå. July 2012

(LISE)

Hello voices

–

Hello Mama
hello Papa

Rolf my love

–

May I be
among your
emotions again

wash me forth
with your gaze

–

Hello friends

So nice to see you here
your arms are glowing

–

Come come

and clarify
me

–

Lend me
the features you have
borne with you

pour out my
colors

–

Must I say it out loud

that I am thinking of life
and so I wander

–

Must I also say

–

that I am missing life

–

But surely you've
already sensed this

–

By my attention

my mood

–

The grass on the heath
is so brittle
tender

the aged
hands yearn
the soul burns

–

Hello Papa

hello Mama

–

Jon-Henrik my
brother and Rolf
my husband

you're missed here

–

You too Sandra
my daughter and
Per my son

–

Even though you are
still here

–

In the light I could
see Rolf again upon
the rocky beach

–

Now I'm no longer
sure if it really
was him

Or if my
old eyes lie

see what they want to see

–

In summer
I wander alone
through the tundra

my cane in hand

–

In my backpack
I've put coffee and salt
some bread

–

If I catch a fish I'll eat
otherwise not

–

Dear Jon-Henrik

How am I to know
that you're not a
dream I once had

of my own creation

–

So much time
has passed since
we last spoke

–

Life

still beats in me
fingers searching
voice breathing

–

And yet so great is the loss
of what once was

your bodies

–

Mama

who sensed me
coming

–

You were the first
woman in the family

–

to give birth in the confines
of a Western
hospital

–

Why did it make you so
sad to give birth to
me Mama

Just because I wasn't
a boy
like Jon-Henrik

–

I remember

when you cut
my hair

–

You said it didn't
much matter

it would grow
long again

–

I stretch out
on the grass with
my backpack on

to recover
a bit

–

It's not far
to the creek now

–

The cold one by the
old reindeer herder cairn

where Papa and
I would get
into such long talks

–

My legs quake

when I lean
over to scoop
up water

–

And can't I just
hear Papa saying:

If you stop
for a drink
at every stream

–

you'll never get
to where you're going

–

Once I ask
him out here
on the tundra

it was up
by the gorge where
one can find
ferns

–

Why Mama
had so wanted
another son

We didn't have
any reindeer to
care for after all

–

Gaisu-Lise
Papa said and smiled

you think too
much

–

But still wasn't I

the one

–

Who slid
Sandra's wedding ring
on her finger

–

Who sent Per out
into this hallowed
bright room

That I'd
prepared for him

–

Maybe

–

I'm aware of how
plain my admiration
for Per has been

And how differently
I've perceived you Sandra

–

You've always said
this is because you
unlike Per

will one day turn into me

–

I know that I
should have talked
to you

When you as if duty-bound
stayed together with your
first love

–

Who you met
when you were sixteen

and are still
married to

–

But I said nothing

–

Not a word did I share
about myself

–

Even though the years
coursed through me like
black paint

when you said you
were moving in together

–

And not a word
about myself did I share
with you Per

–

When you said
you'd taken on a new
driving schedule

And would only be
seeing your daughter on
the weekends

–

My grandchild Jasmin

who reminds me
so much of
my mother

–

Who I was
forced to leave at
the age of seven

I had to leave
my life behind

–

when will I return

–

Oh how I missed
you Ieddne when I was
at the residential school

oh how I missed
you Áhttje

–

Oh how you missed Rolf
Per

when he was
off working

–

In Vietas or
Akkats

VIII

Christmas break. 1956

(LISE)

So subdued

Jon-Henrik had become

–

Lying dismal
at home on
the pull-out sofa

turning the pages
of his comic book

–

I watched him
mouth the words

and I wondered

–

if he'd learned to read

–

What was it that I
sensed behind that
proud hull

What was the life
I saw glide up
into his eyes

–

Then
turn back

slip into
the shadows

–

But not before
giving that somber
cast to his face

like the reindeers' somber
brown gazes

–

The two tame reindeer
that we had last summer

–

They'd walked here

and grazed outside
the window

–

Papa had said

–

That it was torture
for them with the midges
and the heat

and that they would
rather be strolling high
in the fells

–

Jon-Henrik don't
you remember

how we would
talk out in the pasture

–

Lying on each our own
patch of flattened
grass that the reindeer
had ruminated

–

How the grass
was as smooth
as a silky cloth

–

And the earth
rested coolly against
the body

don't you
remember anything

–

I crossed
the floor and sat
down by you

With the doll I'd gotten
for Christmas on my lap

–

Didn't you miss

didn't you think of
us out there

–

What
had changed
since last summer

–

Other than you
not living here
anymore

and the tame reindeer
having all been slaughtered

–

Turned to meat in my mouth

–

And eerie
bloodstains in the snow

one morning when I
walked out

–

By the fire Papa
wrested off his shoes and
one sock

–

He took out his knife
and started scraping
something off his shoe

–

Hey Jonne
he said

–

in his usual
soft voice

–

Now that we don't have
any tame reindeer on
our plot

you're not considered
a Swedish smallholder anymore
but a Lapp

–

So come autumn it's
the residential school
in Jokkmokk for you

Same goes
for you Lise

–

He reached out with his knife

and gently rapped
the doll's head
which was hollow
and dead

–

Jon-Henrik said
nothing

–

He kept flipping
through his
comic book

and I heard
Mama say

–

That there was one thing
she was happy about

–

At least we'd
have each other

out there

IX

The crossing. The start of the school year. 1957

(LISE)

Jon-Henrik won't
you hold my
hand again

if I promise
to stop crying

–

Have you been here before

How long are we going
to stand here waiting on
this bridge

–

Did you recognize
the men who brought us
here on the boat

are you freezing too

–

Can you explain
what's going
to happen next

–

Please don't go anywhere

–

Will we
be taking that
big boat too

Didn't they say that someone
would pick us up here

–

No

those people
look like Sámi

–

Aren't those the
Kuhmunen
girls

and their dad

–

They're wearing
their kolts too
Do you dare go talk
to them

Did you see
it was their dad who
tied their caps

–

Is that the boat

that will take us
to the other side

–

There's swaying under my feet

–

A gentle wind is
teasing my hair
it's playing with my shawl

lifting the fringes
that Mama
has pressed

–

Please can't we
keep traveling
like this

and never again
go ashore

–

No

–

I want to go with my brother

I don't want to go into
the cellar alone

–

And why aren't we allowed
to use the big door

No

–

You don't need
to scrub me

it's tearing up my skin

–

The Kuhmunen sisters
are shy too

without any clothes on

–

But I do what they do

use my hands to cover up

–

No you're wrong

–

My Mama promised

that I'd get to sleep
in my brother's room

X

Much later

(LISE)

The Swedish
language grew
along my thoughts

–

The Sámi since long
asleep in the body
of shame

obedience overlaid

–

Clamped
shut up inside

The voice stirred
barely perceptible
almost impossible
to rouse

–

The Swedish history
of power-hungry kings
mighty great nations

lifted the entire class
toward worship
closer to worship

–

But of our own
history not a word
was written

–

As if our
parents and we
had never existed

had never shaped
anything

–

My heart saw

a ruling body
remove itself from
the world of bodies

–

A hero's
ruling body

–

I was not
dismissive of
that radiant
body

Not resistant
in the face of the mighty

–

The instinct to adapt
was strong

tumbling from my chest

–

While the ruler's
eye gnawed its way
into my life

right through my time

–

A wide-open
child-body

Having lived
for years in its
conquerors' house

–

Recast by
its great

gazing halls

XI

The Nomad Residential School, Jokkmokk, Norrbotten County.
Spring 1958

(LISE)

Tired from waiting

With my forehead
to the window

I had seen how
Mama was the last
to finally get off the bus

–

Behind me Anne
started crying

and we comforted her

–

Neither her mom
nor her dad
was to be seen

among the grown-ups
out there

–

Tense we waited

Nervous the whole day
as our parents were
being shown around

–

In the refectory I was
left on my own
to choke down
the Swedish food

–

Everyone else had
already eaten up
had been excused
from the table

–

I could hear them
running
romping around
the schoolyard

–

Where I too
was let loose

To bring forth
the same strained
spirited din

–

As if we were
showing off

for our dressed-up
parents

–

Now and then

their faces
appeared in the
tall windows

the same ones
we'd looked through
that morning

–

Time slithered as if
across gravel

–

But I let Anne
win my
large steel taw

–

The sky clouded over

and I latched
onto my
mother's neck

–

Wove my
fingers into her hair

–

My arms

–

curled around the
sweet smoky heat
of her body

–

Had we ever
hugged like this Mama

I don't think so

–

She said:

Now show me
where you sleep

and I pointed
out the bed

–

In silence she looked

at the identical
small stools

–

Where we'd neatly
fold up
our clothes

night after night

–

There was so much
I wanted to tell
her

–

How I'd thought that
reindeer herders' children
already knew what to do

when living away
from their parents

–

But they'd cried
in the beginning too

–

Like I'd
cried that first
night

when the night watch
tricked me

–

She'd said
that I could
call home

–

Only
to laugh
at me when

receiver in hand
I realized

–

That we didn't have
a telephone
back home

–

Mama sat calmly
by my narrow bed

–

She listened so
patiently

to every word I
didn't say

–

I tried to sense
what she was thinking

–

I wondered if

Jon-Henrik had told
her

—

that one of the boys
could be mean

About none of us having
our own earmark

—

But I wasn't
about to ask

—

Because she might go
back to the boys' room

and sit with
him instead

—

I promise I won't

I heard her
say before I
fell asleep

—

I promise to
spend the night
with you here

–

But when I
woke up in the dark
the chair was empty

–

And I knew right away

that she had taken
something with her
when she left

–

But I could not
figure out
what it was that
was gone

XII

Places along the Great Lule River Valley. 1970–1974

(LISE)

Again and again
the ocean rises

sluicing from
the body what
has come to pass

–

sweeping tracks
from the sand

–

But the pieces
that loosened from
the cliff

are already gone

–

The hollows
grow ever larger

with each wave
that crashes in

–

The river climbed
silently up the hills

as soon as Vattenfall
whistled it came
creeping:

–

Streamed backwards
up its deep channel and
drowned the earth

When the great
Suorva Dam for the third
time was to be regulated

–

Entreaty

shone from Mama's
eyes

–

She explained
clearly to the Swedes

that the fishing will suffer
if the water rises

–

There was probably
no one who understood
what she was saying

–

And jaws clenched

–

While their hands
polished it all off

dug in and set
to work

–

It was in a classroom
in Malmberget

–

I heard the teacher
talk yet again
about the People's Home

about Sweden's
renowned solidarity

–

While Mama
and Papa were left
to climb their hills

–

Trying to guess how
high the river
would rise

before they began to
tear down the house

–

And the currents come
they break up the earth

rip out roots and
rinse away trails

–

But farthest down
close to the bottom

perhaps
what is oldest and
muddiest

–

remains

–

On its surface
the driving waves

they flowed and played
drew people
to them:

–

More manpower
was needed

–

After the social
studies lesson

I went with the others
to sit on the
gymnasium floor

–

Almost all of
Malmberget's students
had been dismissed
from class

–

To participate
in the miners'
strike meeting

–

Someone had heard
that Olof Palme
was coming

that he would travel
all the way up here

–

To the mining company's
and Vattenfall's world

the one that he
himself had helped
build

–

It is what
he is guarding

It is all that
he can see

–

The mine boss's voice

flowed wildly above the
crowded hall which was
hot with bodies

–

His voice was so robust
his conviction
so intense

–

I glanced at Anne
who was sitting beside me
leaning against
the wall bars

and she smiled back at me

–

Soon we would
be leaving school too

–

And could start working
join the union

–

You took the job you wanted
that's all there was to it

–

Switchboard cleaner or cook

with the old folks at
the Pioneer
or the children
in day care

–

Later the scouring mop
glides lukewarm through
the power plants

I caress

–

the corridors

–

The woman who trains
me as a cleaner
is called Erna

—

When I come
out of the changing room
in the morning

I can hear the ops workers'
yearning young voices
behind me

—

Don't tell Erna
one whispers
but we call her
the Figure Eight

—

All she does is cruise
into the break room

draw an eight on
the floor with her mop
and turn right back around

—

I empty
my bucket and wring
out the rags

—

I spend the weekend
up at Mama
and Papa's

–

I stand with Jon-Henrik

–

Watching the river
flow murky
across the slope

–

That brushy slope

where he and I
used to go
it's underwater now

–

How are our tracks
ever to be heard

Among the Swedes'
roads and
power stations

–

It's Jon-Henrik
who says this

he had also
been drawn down
to the dam

–

To work
for Vattenfall as soon
as school was done

–

I'm surprised
when he says

That he'd preferred to have
taken up with the reindeer

–

Been elected into the
Sámi community

And learned to guide
that wandering gray
soft ocean

across the world
of the fells

–

Just as the lot of us
were once taught
at the Nomad School
that this is what the Sámi do

that this is how
we all live

–

He laughs
and says:

–

Who knows what
the spring flood
will bring with it

this drowned
earth may yet
be fertile

–

Do you remember when
Ester Tomma
washed ashore
right down there

After having
drifted around
behind the dam
for ten whole years

–

And I said:

–

Aren't you morbid

–

It was too soon
to say anything

about what
had taken root in my
own plots

–

The sea rises

remixes worlds
weaves in souls

–

Oh how I had
burned

my arms in flames

–

that damn mop
was in our way in the closet

–

Oh how I had
hungered
for him

–

His name was Rolf

he came from a village
near Boden

–

Down there he said
I dammed over my
own childhood home

–

We hike in Muddus

I smoke a cigarette
feel our child kicking
hiccuping

–

Rolf lies on the blanket
drinking a beer

–

The paths under
me are alive

have memories

–

Inside my belly
skin is drawn

–

it is shaped in life

–

One weekend we
make the long journey
to Aunt Ella's spot
on the hill

–

I'm wearing a
new floral tunic

and when she catches sight
of me she shouts:

–

From where I'm standing
you look like
a gypsy

–

During the week I clean
the Swedes' power plant

While Mama
and Papa farther
upstream have to
spend hours

–

Picking from the net
scraps of fish
shredded

by branches and
drowned woods

–

Because Vattenfall

–

didn't bother to
clear the hills

before the river rose

–

At last the weekend
so free
quiet

commuters fade
from the village

–

Only when we're lying
on the bed do I sense
how tired I am

my back pain

–

At the Christmas party
the boss asks the women
to dance by saying:

May I have this dance
even though you've got
such ugly breasts

–

I just smiled
when he joked
with me

glided along in the dance
unable to act and
at a loss

–

But it did not roll
right off me

–

I walk across the dam
breathe in the spring air

–

In the river
the current generates
crackles mysteriously

I watch a seagull rise

–

Summer

it will be summer

–

At first I didn't know
what to say around
Rolf's friend Malte

–

I never thought I'd
become like a
child again

so nervous

–

As insecure as I
was at Nomad

–

The gleaming
summer nights
filled with
the dusky scent
of blossom

the taste of
succulent earth

–

It was before the winter

when Rolf was to start
working off-site again

–

Alone in Porjus
I wondered if we existed
if it was real

Was he seeing someone
else

–

Who was
doing the cleaning

the cooking up there

–

Salt and smoke
was the taste of Mama's
dried meat

which I saved for
Rolf in the fridge

–

Strong and healthy

the child brushed
against my stomach

–

Oh how happy I was
after I'd given birth

Rolf is crying

–

Give her to Daddy now
he can bathe her
let's you and I go out
on the fire escape
for a smoke

said the midwife
at my delivery

–

A Swede called Britta

Britta Katarina Persson

–

As a kid I was called
Li'l Småland
after my dad
she told me

–

He was from there

Moved up here
to build
dams

–

Was a machinist first
then a blaster

–

She stubbed out her
cigarette and asked
what our girl
would be called

Can Daddy choose
she said or will you pick
something you know
Lappish

–

And it dawned on me

that we'd never
discussed it

XIII

(ROLF)

To think that Lise said

several years after
we christened Per

–

That she'd never
really liked
that name

–

Just because of some
sheepish man
who'd lived near them
For a few years

while they were
wintering in Porjus

–

Why didn't she
say something right away

she just let me
name my son
after my father

–

We stood by the
sports field

watched the boys
come charging
to tackle Per right as he
got the ball

–

I heard Lise shout:

Just wipe it away Per
get up and keep playing

–

Can't you see
my sister scolded
at Mom's later

Per must be
allergic

–

You saw how his nose
and eyes were
running today

after he took a spill
on the grass

\-

You could at least
take the boy to a doctor
because Lise won't
have the sense to

\-

After all she's afraid
of health care

\-

And I plaster

Per's fresh scrapes
stroke his arms

\-

I hear Mom in the kitchen

dishes clattering

\-

It occurs to me that she
never makes grouse anymore

\-

Not since that time
when Dad was still alive

\-

And they came to visit

he'd suddenly
leaned forward and
told Lise

–

That she was the
only one he knew who
could make good grouse

–

To think how he used to
hunt birds

back when they
had the farm

–

The farm I'd
always thought was just
an empty shimmer

from Papa's childhood

–

But that when I came home

and said that their farm
was next in line to
be dammed over

–

Almost at once
had hardened into
this difficult memory

–

around the river where
the farm had been

–

But also in Papa's body
when later he'd walk around here
with such discomfort

up the stairs
to the apartment

–

To think that Mom
would turn so
kind and soft

when feeding
the dogs
cuddling the cat

–

Per changes the channel
and I can see my
brother before me

in the kitchen
complaining to
Mom

After Dad had
given us some
new chore

–

Fetching wood
or weeding
the potato patch

–

How easy it was
for my brother
to just take a seat

And yet again apply
to be petted by her

–

Did you have fun today
I ask Per who's
almost asleep

But he just shrugs

–

Do your eyes itch a lot
I ask

But he replies:
Dunno

–

What are you saying boys
Mom wonders

Finally coming out
of the kitchen with a towel
in her gray hands

–

And I reply:

Nothing

XIV

In the meeting room. Porjus 2010

(ROLF)

The big boss's eyes
weighed up my
courage

–

It's not working
this isn't possible

I repeated

–

You can't break
our crews up
yet again

you already
did that

–

I saw papers
with numbers in
every hand

–

Management's men
who began to squirm
self-consciously

in their lofty chairs

–

Each time we get
a new boss I said

he does what
you're doing

–

Every single one
has started off
like you

–

Breaking apart our crews
our every routine

As if none
of you can hear what
we're saying

–

Then the boss
calmly gets up
from his chair

–

With feigned
surprise he takes
the floor

exchanges glances
with the others like
a giggly boy

–

With a haughty smile

he looks down on me

–

I could tell that to him
my expertise was
good for nothing

–

In his big boss mind
anyone
could replace me

–

I tossed a pleading glance
at the younger ones

–

The ones who'd promised
to have my back
if only I
spoke first

–

But there they sit

glowering
at the floor

–

So I say:

Do what you want

XV

We sat awhile
in the kitchen

Malte and I

–

We talked about
management and the
new hires on the floor

–

In a few years
being and time would feel
different

We would come
into our lives anew
like two kids

in retirement

–

Binders

from every single course I
took for work

–

They filled the
closet in the hall
which I'd made
into my office nook

–

I could throw them out
right now

What difference
would it make

–

Everything I'd learned
over the years

those forty-plus years
with Vattenfall

–

Was inside of
this existence

–

But it had
lost its meaning
to me now

It was going to be
so easy to leave

–

The young ones are
up to speed

I think they already
know more than we do
Malte said

–

And I thought of Per

telling me that he
would give holding on
to a job another try

–

That he wanted to be more
like Sandra

–

The door opened

and Lise and Sandra
walked in from the garage

–

They both hung
up their jackets

pulled off their shoes

–

I can empty
the dishwasher
I said

and started to get up

–

But Lise shook
her head

–

And Sandra

went into the bathroom

–

There she stood with
the door wide open
doing herself up a bit

she was on her way home

–

To think that beauty's
charm

rested so plainly in
her face
braiding its colors

–

into an image
admired by all

–

She

a queen
among mortals

–

A species of beauty

–

Lise
it's only occurring
to me now

That you never
would have teased
Per so much
about his heritage

–

had he also been
of that species

XVI

At preschool. Porjus. 1984

(ROLF)

I sat and watched as
Per was asked to pass
the water jug

–

Those hunched
shoulders spoke their
own language

As he looked
at the child
who took the jug
from him

without a word

–

because it was no
big thing

–

It was nothing

–

But I saw that our son
hardly dared
pass that jug along

–

Lise what should we do

–

Do you know how to
get the courage to rise

when courage is low

–

On Saturday Per and I
spend a long time
playing in puddles

–

I say that I have to
stop by Malte's house

there's a work order he
wants to talk through

–

Lise scowls

really laying it on
she sighs:

But it's the weekend

–

Sandra looks at us

She starts joking around
with her gloves
putting them on her head

she's so darn cute

–

Everything is in bloom
Vattenfall is expanding

Soon they'll fill
the pool behind the school
with fresh water

As they do
this time of year

–

Along the way I pass
the school building

I see the Social Democrats'
women in the windows
of the cafeteria

–

They're training
there all weekend

Malte had said

\-

The Young Eagles are
hosting some
sort of camp
for the kids

so the women
can take courses

\-

I hear the kids
singing up in
the gym

\-

They're usually taught
to sing workers' songs
to paint placards
for May Day

\-

It's hot

The Milles sculpture
in the park rises
hovers off the grass

\-

The newly poured asphalt
warms the earth

\-

Someone mentioned

that the shooting range
is opening up again
at the weekend

–

Imagine
if Mother-in-law
wanted to come
from the fells to
watch the children

–

Lise and I could
visit the hotel

play badminton
in the old power station

–

You took your time
she says later
while we're
eating dinner

–

Don't you like it
Lise asks

When she notices
that I'm not having
seconds of her
smoked heart

–

That night we scream
at each other

it makes
my body ache

–

Lise cries

–

It's as if all of this
and all of us here

Have been dredged up
to serve you men
who just care for the
power plant

–

And I notice
Sandra

slipping silently
behind our bedroom door

–

I hadn't even
thought about her
being able to hear us

–

I'd almost
forgotten that she existed

XVII

The Swedish Conversation Club. Porjus. Winter 2015

(LISE)

The waves rustle

they turn and
withdraw

–

Life by the river

has often
been like life
in the reeds

–

the reeds by the riverbank
where Moses was placed

–

An awareness that
someone might
unexpectedly arrive

–

and suddenly
exist here

–

I have walked along
the rocky beach

By boat I have taken
myself across the river
to the other side

–

That's as far as
you can go

–

Downstream the dam
stands in the river's way

–

And upstream
the rapids
stop you

–

I've taken the car

followed the asphalt where
it has been spread

–

Roads that ran between
the Swedes' power stations
and mines

to which so many
people had come

–

Blown ashore

to then put down roots

–

Here in this haphazard
garden

high up in the river valley

–

The German deserter
who Papa
would talk about

–

The one who came
wandering across
the fell one evening

all the way from the
Norwegian side

–

One winter when Papa
was young

–

Barefoot in the snow
the soldier had shouted
that his feet were burning

–

And the American
draft dodger

who boarded with Mama
and me in the fells
when Sandra was small

–

Rolf was about to leave for
the summer to work in Vietas

when that young
American arrived

–

With the tourist boat

–

The man had been
called up for Vietnam
but fled

He boarded with us
for a few weeks

–

We taught him to weave
Sámi bands that he
would sell to tourists

–

He was warm
he said that
I was warm

behind the rocks

–

Sandra had lain in the grass

Eaten cloudberries and
dried meat from Mama's
cutting board

which she had brought
out with her

–

Outside the window
it's snowing now

–

And people
have begun blowing
this way again

After all these years
of thinning out

–

When all they did
was drift away

After Vattenfall
withdrew

–

Now they're whirling
up this way again

–

I put on the down jacket
Sandra gave me
zip it up

Then I walk down
the hill to the conversation club

–

Bibbi's already there

I think she looks
the same as she did
back at Nomad

–

But of course I know
we're over the hill
to them

to the young people
who've moved here

–

Over two hundred
refugees came to Porjus

Until then there were
three hundred and fifty
of us living here

–

I try to talk
with a young man

I want to say that he
looks like my Per

–

Per who's only ever
on the road

in his truck

–

But my English
won't stretch

–

Then I sit a long time
and search his face

For signs
of dreams imagination
and calm

–

I think
I find traces
of violence

but I don't know

–

And then I think
I see

–

something I recognize
from my own life

–

In Bibbi's high
closed hard
face

sitting across
from me like
a leaden shield

–

And around her
heart as well

–

Bibbi
have you also done
everything you can

–

To never
be taken for dumb
or primitive

for someone who
let themselves
be conquered
and has been too
obedient

–

The door opens

And in comes
a cousin of Bibbi's who
takes a seat at the table

–

They speak such a
lovely Sámi

–

It's the same dialect
that was spoken back home
on our hill

–

The language that
still existed when
we started school

Jonne and I

–

Am I that dumb

that I can't manage
to keep my own
language alive

–

I just let it slip away

be driven from my children

–

So now Sandra
sounds like a book
no dialect at all

Trying
as a grown woman
to learn Sámi
with her children

–

I can't get a sound
out those many times
she says:

Answer me in Sámi
Mama

–

And I want to share this

With that young
man sitting at

the table next to Bibbi

with his coffee cup
and cinnamon bun

–

But all I can do is smile
and he smiles back

nods knowingly
raises his cup

–

Does he know that I'm
sitting here listening
to his language

–

Between the words
that are no more than sounds
to me

and which I
do not understand

–

I can sense something
he has left behind
has lost

–

and that he does

not want to do without

–

Will he also
have a child here
at some point

Which language will
his grandchildren
get to speak

–

Which birds and trees
will they learn
the names of

and which songs
will they sing

–

About sun and wind

war and men

–

rich and poor

XVIII

River

that you can run so dark
there beside the road

–

A gliding shifting
deep veil
heavy

across a bed of rock

–

You sealed fortress
of water and cold

when do you imagine
letting my child in

–

Allowing her to
fasten somewhere

like you did
with Malte's son

—

Will only the boys
be given jobs here

—

Never again
do I want to see the sorrow that
rises in Sandra's eyes

When she comes to visit

—

and through the
kitchen window
hears the cars

Of young
line installers
and operations
workers

—

Which they park
by the grill
where they can afford to
have lunch every day

—

I remember
when we were new
to Porjus

Rolf would have
lunch at nine o'clock

–

They went to work
at six and took lunch
at nine

a coffee break around one

–

Then in the seventies
lunch was moved
to eleven

–

How many times
hasn't the radio
been the one
to tell me

that new facts
had been established

–

That I had always
been a danger to
my own children

just because I smoke
and am overweight
and uneducated

–

I have heard it said
so many times

–

That the children in this
country with the greatest
risk of facing
hardship

have mothers
like me

people such as we
have been Rolf

–

Can't you help
Sandra out with a job Rolf

something at the workshop
or in the joinery

–

If only I could
reroute Porjus so
that she is needed

until something here takes
her by the arm and
puts her to use:

–

Heart and
lungs

kidneys and
liver

–

Legs that must
be allowed to stride forward
and a head that wants
to think thoughts

while the hands
shape
do things

–

But Sandra
you should know

this purse right here
will never be empty

–

My own mother said
this to me once
too:

–

That this purse right here
Lise

it will never be empty

–

She had squatted down

I could not remember
her ever having
brought her face
so close to me before

–

She took out her pocketbook

One of those wide
leather pocketbooks
an accordion model

Its many compartments
expanded

–

And like an incantation

she had said
those words

XIX

In the kitchen. Pentecost 1973

(LISE)

It's called Blue Danube

says Britt-Marie
as I unwrap
the paper

–

A teapot
cups and plates made of
blue-patterned porcelain

–

I say thank you and
feel her soft
back against my hands
warm under her blouse

as we hug

–

Then I carefully fold
up the wrapping paper
put it in the closet

–

From inside the room
I hear Rolf sit down
with the others

–

He says that it
was one of his
work friend's
mothers

who usually handled
the funerals
in the Communists'
little chapel

–

A small gray building
at the far end of
the churchyard

which Grandmother
kept away from

–

And was built
for those who didn't want
to be buried by the priest

–

I hear him laugh

and think again that
Rolf is not me

–

Even now

–

though so many
years have passed since I
graduated from Nomad

I only need to shut my eyes
to wander out among
God's angels

dancing in circles

–

Yellow trumpets
to their mouths

–

I can hear the sound
of their rustling mantles
as they file into some
verdant kingdom of heaven

on one of the cardboard posters

–

nailed to the wall
in every classroom

–

I remember when I
met Rolf

–

I was still sure that
you'd get a lightning bolt
to the head

if you disavowed God

–

At Nomad the
Læstadian girls wore shawls
to hide their hair

–

And when Mama once
heard that a little first cousin
of mine wasn't going to be baptized

it became to her a
child of sorrow

–

Who was going to hell

where several of the Læstadian
girls' parents were
also going

–

The earnest Læstadian
girls

who weren't allowed to look
at themselves in the mirror

–

Who surely suffered
from the knowledge that
their parents had already
as children
been damned

because they'd made
themselves
guilty of mortal sin

–

In the tent schools
in the twenties

Where one summer they
let themselves be
photographed
naked

by the racial biologist

–

Because the teacher
and the priest had convinced
their families

That the parliamentary
decision these
so-called scientists
had invoked

to get them to
undress for those pictures
had to be followed

–

Pictures
they would
never get to see

And would never
find out what they
were for

–

In the morning
we wake early
drink strong coffee

–

Hear Uncle Ernst
treading around in
the apartment below us

Before he turns
the key
tramps into the stairwell

–

Then he knocks awhile
on our door

Some article in *Flamman*
has probably upset him

—

and now he needs to
discuss it

—

But we don't
want to be home

we disappear
under the covers

—

Later in the evening
Rolf and Malte talk for ages

mostly about work

—

We sit in the kitchen

and I fill our new cups
with coffee

—

There's knocking
at the door again

But this time it's not Ernst
it's Papa

—

It's the first time
he has stopped by
for a visit
on his own

–

I see him at rest
bringing the cup
to his mouth

As Rolf and he
start talking about someone
they both know

–

Right as I get
up to put
on more coffee

I hear

–

Malte saying to Rolf:

By the way do you know
how to tell a girl is a Lapp
just by looking at her

–

Well her slit runs
crossways instead
of down the middle

and he laughs

–

But Rolf doesn't laugh

–

Nor does he see
the temper in
Papa's eyes

XX

Stuor Stuodak Mountain, Gällivare,
Norrbotten County. Fall 1975

(LISE)

When Papa is on his deathbed

he asks me to help
him get home

–

He's been cared for
awhile at the hospital
in Gällivare

–

He seems so
completely
occupied

by his own
concentration

–

On what
I do not know

–

But it makes me
not want to interrupt

–

Jon-Henrik and I
have been smuggling
beer in to him
for several days now

–

We dress him in
warm clothes

–

As usual we say
that we're going
for a stroll and take
him with us

get him in the car

–

Mama didn't want
to help

She says
it's too taxing

–

Fall's cool
mist sinks gray
through the air

settles in the grass
gleams on
the rocks

–

We've got Papa
on the ATV

We make our slow way
to the lake

–

Then there he lies
in the wilted grass

gazing at the water

–

I sit on a rock

–

Let my fingers wander
across the rugged
rock-skin under me

while the nature
around us gently
ferries me off

–

To a starker
landscape

–

That might exist too

–

It is high up
on the Norwegian coast

–

Great boulders
lie there rattling
against each other

And the Atlantic winds
blow through the crevices
between the rocks

–

I can hear them
playing on the coast

as if on a
colossal organ

–

Papa died
that day

we never thought
it would
happen

–

He gets stiff and
far too heavy for
Jonne and me

–

And we have to arrange
for the seaplane
to come

take him
down for us

–

His shrouded
body does not fit
in the plane

–

We end up having to
strap him
to one pontoon

–

What was I to
say to Rolf

what was I to
say to our children

–

How am I to
tell stories about life

–

Without becoming the
eccentric Sámi

Making jokes
at my own
expense

–

How am I to
explain to them

that the ruin
is in my voice

XXI

Porjus. Summer 1977

(LISE)

Rolf and I
we bought Mama
a life vest

–

After Papa
had died she kept
on fishing alone
up in the fells

but she didn't want
to put it on

–

I'm not about to float
around in the water
freezing to death
is what she said

–

But I'll tie
my handbag
to the boat

So you can fish
the money out
if I fall in

–

Mama

come for a visit
I begged

–

I said that Jonne
was coming and
might eat with us

so then she came along

–

In the car she refuses
as usual to
buckle up

–

But she holds
the seat belt
across her lap

in case the police
pass by

–

So she won't get a fine

—

Her restless steps
in the kitchen
is it hot in here
she says

—

Once more she asks
when Jon-Henrik
is coming

—

And if I know
when he'll next be
up in the fells

where he now has
his handful of reindeer

—

I wonder how
it's going for him
she says

He has it good
don't you think

—

And I could see
him in front of me

six seven years old

–

He's lying
on the grass
talking with Papa

And is wearing
that sweater she
knitted him

–

With a glossy yarn
that shone
in the sun

the one on which it said
The Son

–

After we finish eating
he calls to say that
he isn't coming

–

And I scoop
his portion into a
lunch box for Rolf

stick it in the freezer

–

Something smells
Mama says

and goes outside to
get some air

–

When she comes back in

she's already arranged
a ride homeward along the river
with some Swedes

–

She says she can
walk the final stretch

–

And I send a
pack of cigarettes
with her

–

So she'll have
something to do

XXII

Distribution of the estate. Fall 1983

(LISE)

You have to say something
Jon-Henrik

I can't make
every decision myself

–

What should we do
with Mama's things

–

Muddy empty
plastic drums

the red and yellow
tubs we kept
the nets in

–

Mattresses and
car tires

–

The blankets
Papa had taken from
the Swedish Tourist Association
were surely in there too

moldering
slowly away

–

In the shed behind the
little house in Porjus

where Rolf and I
finally got
Mama to move

–

It was near to where
there was still
a shantytown
from pioneer times
back when we first met

–

But we don't need to
do anything yet do we
Jon-Henrik said

and I looked down
at the grass

–

I said that we should
get to grips with it now

before he made his way
into the fells

–

But he just

shrugged

–

Then ambled
back to the house

where the two heaps
of coffee packets
were waiting for us

–

It was the coffee we
divvied up first

Toward the end
Mama was buying
more and more coffee
almost every day

–

Should we divvy up
the money too
I said

–

And my brother looked
at me with surprise

—

But I already knew

that Mama hadn't said
anything to him about
where the money was

—

So we're standing outside
the shed again

We'd walked the same
path that Mama
and I had taken
that time

—

I search the wall

for the marking
lowest down by the
dry grass

—

She'd said
that if the house catches
fire Susanna

well there's
nothing in there

—

But behind this wall

double-plastic-bagged
is where I've hidden
the money

–

This is where you
plant the axe and chop
a hole

–

Did you know
I ask Jonne

that she went back
to calling me Susanna
toward the end

–

And I watch him
shake his head

–

as he lets me press the
grimy bags into his arms

–

Have you heard that
the priest secretly
gave Sandra's daughter
my last name

I say

–

It was at the baptism
last spring

–

He'd thought
it would be
too sad

if that name
were to die out
as well

XXIII

The names resound

they lift like wings
from the children's mouths
are written on the books
that the teacher handed out

–

She stands alone at the window

watching spring's
slow approach
listening to the child

–

Who is reading aloud
to the others

–

It's one of the
older girls

–

By now the teacher has realized

that this is Lise's
and Sandra's
Ella-Susanna

–

Lise
her classmate
at the Nomad School

–

To think how often
they played together
there

what fun they had

–

Lise who yoiked
so beautifully for her
behind the shed

–

She looks up
to see Lise's
grandchild

–

Hears the Sámi being born
and becoming as if
of and unto itself

in this somehow newly
ignited body

–

With a voice so
self-evident

–

With hands that can glow
so young and warm
when holding the book

it makes her wipe
her own hands
on her pant legs

–

To rid them of
the old

–

The blue in her
gray fingers

that she can no longer
witness alone

–

Old hands like
snow heavy as snow

–

Must I really
watch them
melt away

she thinks

–

Should I arm
these children
for battle

Against future
realms

Ædni

I

Gällivare. Easter 2016

(SANDRA)

With courage
I have worn my
kolt today

–

I hang it
out to air

–

My children are sleeping

suspect nothing

–

In discussions
and meetings
we fight

the kolt and I

–

With its colors
it opens up
the Swedes' eyes

brooches
rattle
they beam upon
my breast

–

An of-woman-sewn
armor of broadcloth
and silver

–

It calls upon them
to regard me

When I speak
on my children's
behalf

–

Now they're sleeping
soundly
on soft pillows
unknowing

we play in
the world
my children
and I

–

But the kolt stands
at the ready

–

For each new
growth ring it
will fight

for every
cracked branch
of the family tree

–

it will bear witness
and remember

–

There it hangs

already awaiting
the next blow

–

My children

Never will you
need to ask
never will you
wonder

about
your lineage

–

I bring my kolt indoors

press it hard
to my heart

–

There my skin is

steeped
of gleaming color

–

Armed with roots
and life

II

Gällivare District Court. February 3, 2016

(SANDRA)

Today I saw a
hope be born

light
clear

–

In the eyes of the
Sámi village's
chairman

when he read that
shining verdict

–

He wrapped his arms
around his daughter

on the verge of tears
the two of them

–

And this hope

also brushed against
me as I stood

–

In the warm
waiting room

Among the folks
from Girjas

–

Brooches glinting
like pure gold
on the women's shawls

–

But the kolt

–

as ever urged on the fight

–

Don't stand around
going soft

The State would
never let the Sámi
community win

–

There's no chance the judge
will let this victory
go all the way

to the Supreme Court

–

And the hope wilted
shriveled

–

A spring leaf in my hand

so brittle

–

The branchwork of
history finely
embedded

–

Mama had said

that considering how
the State's attorneys
behaved during
this land rights trial

–

She didn't think
reconciliation was
possible

—

Alone in the car

deep in thought I drive
homeward

—

The snowflakes
weightless

sailing

—

The gas station's
signs dingy
with soot

Almost illegible
in the waning light

—

I see the birch trees'
twisted charcoal
eyes

—

From the roadside
ditch

rises the raw
earthy scent
of cold

–

On the electricity box
fighting words

Spray-painted there
by Sámi youth

–

At home I take
off the kolt

I fold
up the shawl

–

Place the large
brooch in the
jewel box
on the dresser

next to the smaller
one with gold-plated
leaves

–

I wish my
Uncle Jonne
had lived

to hear this

–

Which rights will be
won back next
which stolen crania
and disavowed
crimes

–

We have so much
left to win

–

I'd promised to
call Mama up so I type
in her number but
change my mind

I call Andreas
instead

–

out in the reindeer
woods

to tell him

–

He doesn't answer

–

I call
my brother up

he doesn't answer

III

Second day of the Girjas trial. May 2015

(SANDRA)

The man

on the podium
in front of us

–

Said that all
archaeological
material that Girjas
has adduced

is irrelevant

–

This came right after
the State's lawyers
refuted

our status as an
ethnic group

–

Has Sweden
changed its mind then

–

Didn't they attest
to us being
an Indigenous people

Is this fact no longer
protected by
the constitution

–

Mama has made up
the big bed for us

she plays with the children
changes them
out of their clothes

–

So to put them to bed
tonight

since I can't manage

–

Warily I stroke
my boy's forehead

pull a hair out of
the girl's mouth

–

I take in
their cheekbones

their eyelids

–

Which stories has
Mama left for them
little balls of yarn

–

For them to squeeze
along the way

follow and unravel

–

With their sensitive
hands that
grasp everything

reading the air and
the slightest mood

–

Mama what I
encountered today

–

If you'd seen those
men on the jury
their age

–

What do you think
they were taught about
the Sámi in school

–

How much time will
Girjas's lawyer have to
explain to them

All the things that
they as adults have
not found out
for themselves

–

Before they stop
listening

lose interest

–

They'll have to
excuse us
if we disrupt their
dreams

they'll have to
forgive us

–

But the era
of progress
and the world's
conscience

314

does not contain
the full
history of their land

–

Our land

of course is one
they've never
even seen

–

Do they even know
how we have been
removed between
four nations

–

Even though our land

this ground right
here that we named
long ago

–

Has always stretched
right across northern
Scandinavia and into the
Kola Peninsula

–

So they'll have to
forgive us

if we turn
their maps on them

–

Isn't it about time
that their children
also learn to hear
the voices

of our shared
history

–

You Nordic children
who have gone forth
so lightly

As if you were
entirely without power
without a past

–

Those who have
gone before you
apparently
forgot

to pack your baggage

IV

The trial's first day. Out in the reindeer pasture

(SANDRA)

Once
here shone
a colder sun

the bygone
winters' sun

–

Nowadays
we struggle
with the thaw

the melt

–

The cold comes

And the snow cover
turns to rock
half-melted after
a mild spell

–

So Andreas is forced
to set out again in this
forest fused with ice

impenetrable
and hard

–

To the reindeers'
searching gray lips

so he can supplement
their feed

–

Slipping hooves
that scratch and
claw at the ice

as they walk
and starve

–

Few of the usual
winter grazing grounds
can be trusted
anymore

With these mild
then suddenly
ice-cold winters

that bewilder all life

–

I stand with our girl
in Andreas's new
reindeer pasture

Among
last year's calves
as shadows

–

Their shadows in this
weather of oblivion

–

where their food is not

–

Andreas just called
They're driving the
does out toward a
new area

where there might be
more bare earth

–

He said that they'll
have to find their own
way east

–

And there could be
other groups that have
already taken up there

–

But what is there to do

–

They'd have to
turn right back around

maybe head
west again

–

To think Dad's father
had to watch all those reindeer
disappear into the lake
Ella-Susanna says

that time the herd crashed
through the ice

–

That early spring
up by Kutjauri Lake

–

Tired we wander
homeward from
the pasture

Ella-Susanna
and I

–

She had seen
a curious doe
prise out

–

A new leaf
a tiny
coil

–

Among the weaklings
we had gathered
last winter

in order to save
their lives

–

Though their stomachs
are too sensitive
for fodder

–

Downcast and faint
I walk ahead
through the forest
on the road

the phone rings again

–

I answer and
hear Mama who

starts talking
right away

–

How nice

to simply listen
awhile

–

To feel the
thoughts
release

–

be shuffled off

–

By someone
else's thoughts

–

After some time
has passed

I make sure
to ask her about
my father-in-law's name
his real one

–

Andreas was so
unsure when we wrote
the obituary

–

Once Father-in-law
told me

that his name
was Nils-Ola
I say

–

But Andreas says
it was Nils-Olof

–

And Mama says
that she doesn't know

She'd always
called him Nille

–

Should we have used
the Tax Agency's spelling
of his last name
I continue

Even though
it's wrong

–

Or was it a nice thing
to write out Father-in-law's
last name using the correct
Sámi spelling

–

Mama thinks
it would have been a
better bet to use
the one from
the Tax Agency

–

Then we sit awhile
in the kitchen

talking about the day

–

Ella-Susanna fixes
sandwiches
at the counter

and I tune in to
the Sámi radio station

–

The trial has begun

Girjas Sámi Village is
suing the Swedish State

–

Someone is saying

that the question
of ethnicity
is not relevant

–

Nomads are one thing
and Lapps another

they say in court

–

This is the State's
attorney speaking

–

Again and again
she calls us
Lapps

And I notice
that I'd forgotten

–

It's been so long
since I heard someone
use that hateful word

–

I wonder if Per
is listening too

–

He does often listen
to the radio in the truck
when he's
on the road

–

I sit still
on the kitchen sofa
and wait awhile

clearing my head
gathering myself

–

Then I say to
Ella-Susanna who
has heard everything:

–

Come on
put on your kolt

–

We have to go
to the trial

V

A little later along route E4

(PER)

Sandra calls

to tell me how
the State's attorneys
jeer at Girjas
when they assert
their rights

–

Because they aren't
based on
written documents

like those that make up
Swedish culture

–

But on oral sources
archaeological sources and
the ground's sources

–

The ground's every trace
of presence
action and life

Which she says
with a commanding voice

–

How is it that
she turned out to be
the confident one

–

I can't help
that I sometimes
wonder

How she turned out
the way she turned out

–

A confident
brazen Sámi
queen

sure of everything and
full of answers

–

Sleeps with her armor
strapped on

–

To think I don't
remember when she
was crowned

when she made this decision

—

To learn Sámi
and sew kolts
while I was driving
around as if
in a fog

in a truck that
isn't mine

—

And on roads
that are not my
roads

—

What do these
things have to do
with my life

—

Manal my love
do you remember

I tried to go
down into the mine
to work like you do

—

It meant getting
to spend more time

at home with you
and Jasmin

–

But I couldn't
hack it

it was like
with Papa and
Vattenfall

–

Down underground
with people who talk
and coffee breaks

rules and meetings

–

Sandra says

That they might start
driving the herd like
they used to

so they can do
without
a scooter

–

But hasn't she
been listening

–

To the old-timers
when they talk about
how hard it was

On skis in the ice
and snow

–

As for me
I count hours
minutes

–

Along the row of
streetlamps and
taillights

roving in the dark

–

A monotone whisper
sends me to sleep

–

Until the man
in the truck behind
me suddenly
overtakes

with such
terrible speed

–

I grab the wheel

fear
pounding

–

Later at the gas
station

there are already
several switched-off
truck cabs with others in
need of sleep

–

Inside at the register
I ask

about the lending
shelf with
audiobooks
for us drivers

–

He says no

they don't have
one anymore

–

And I ask why
the library
took it away

But he
doesn't know

VI

The men are to construct a scaffold.
The hospital in Gällivare. 2005

(PER)

That time the
shelter dispersed
and loneliness
burned in me:

–

Tiptoeing
behind Papa
that big boy

can't sort himself out

–

Body made
of veils where
barbs snag

–

Per when will you
finally toughen up

–

Start to reign like we do

–

Mocking looks
and words that scald
from men I'm supposed to
work with every day

–

But I followed Papa

let him go first

–

Guide me around
among the men

watchful like him
and opinionated

–

Then I found him
so small and crushed

Left in a hospital bed
stitched up
and plastered

–

A tender shield
that couldn't take
another blow

–

I wanted to
hold his hand

but I couldn't

–

Mama stood on her own
by the window

–

Quietly touching the
sun-bleached curtain
while she kept
an eye out for
Andreas's car

–

She yawned
and I said:

Do you want
to go out
get some air

–

But she shook
her head

–

I asked
if she wanted
an evening paper

and she nodded

–

I saw Papa struggle
to swallow
in the sleep
where he lay

in his
half-drugged
body

–

Suddenly so much older

His leg in a cast
and a sprinkle
of sand in his
gray hair

–

Couldn't they have
sent one of the younger
ones to climb those
scaffolds I said to
Mama before I left

My courage like ash

–

The next morning
I'd be alone
at work

Me who'd been
transferred to
Papa's crew

–

I'll just have to
suck it up again

–

When Hendrik
rips on me for the whole
lunch hour

–

Torments me because
of my inhaler

like he did every
recess at school

–

He'd heckle
me in Sámi

–

because he knew
I wouldn't understand

VII

In the car that same summer

(PER)

How does a language heal

I suppose you have to start
somewhere

–

Find your way forward letter
by letter
word after word

get to the roots

–

At some point
another voice
emerges

–

But it will be
another

–

Not the same

for that other voice
was not to be

–

The one called
mother tongue

–

Still
how different they are

right from the start

–

The books that
we have open
on our laps

–

Sandra Papa
Mama and I

–

Mine is of longing

Sandra's is warlike

–

And Papa and
Mama hide their
books so well

that I'd never been able
to guess what
is written there

–

But it doesn't matter

–

Mama and I
travel down the road

–

We'd set off
from Porjus early

–

Each time she passes
one of those new
road signs

with the place name
in both Swedish
and Sámi

–

I try to figure out
what it means

–

But I can't decipher
any of the people's and
the land's history

–

If it had perhaps
been thought that
the fell over there

looked like something
in particular

–

Or the stretch
of smooth water
we pass

Might it have been
a good stretch for fishing

or crossing

–

Or if this is where
something happened
a long time ago

That only the place name
still bears witness to
for those who understand

–

I know that Bårjås
means sail of course

everyone knows that

–

But Jåhkåmåhkke
och Jiellevárre

–

That means
Split Mountain
I think

Mama says

–

It must have to
do with that long valley
over there

–

A bit farther on
I see yet another road sign
and sound out the word

Leipojärvi

–

Järvi

isn't that Finnish for lake

–

The sun is still low

And I don't know why
I come to think of Nila
the boy Nila

–

The one who Mama
brought to life for me
when I was small

–

She even drove us
all the way to Piteå
one summer

the whole family

–

To see the mental
hospital where
he had lived

–

That big silent
raging boy
who never learned
to speak

–

And who Mama
herself had never met

–

Except in her own
mother's images
of him

which she had
handed down
to my mother

–

Which she had developed
in my mother

–

as if slowly rinsed
with solvent

–

A long ongoing
stilly bath

of memories
guesswork
and tracks

–

Why had
Grandma conjured
those attrited
features

–

Why dig up
light from earth
light from light

–

time from time itself

–

Mama maybe
I should try
and find out

–

Why I too
can so clearly
see him

VIII

I go out
for a smoke in
the parking lot

–

A stiffening costume

Trying to keep it
together around my brother's
every contorted attempt
to be here with us

–

Those who we both
have always relegated to
the great failure that
I have made space for

and carry within

–

How long does Per imagine
staying in the background
of existence

349

there in the shadows

–

Where blood runs from
the cuts he makes
in the arms of longing

–

With his sensitive fingers

which might still
belong to the place that
was no more when our
lives began

–

Now you're coming
down the road

through the glare of
streetlights

–

And I say
out loud to you Per
that you are brave

–

We order in food
and you start talking

–

The coloration of worry poured

through the eyes

—

For a long while
all I do is listen
to your words

even though our food
is getting cold

—

Feeling the roar
of helplessness

Each time you talk about
harming yourself Per

—

But surely you have
also been able to discern
joy and heat

—

You also find yourself
embattled don't you

—

riding the winds

—

Perhaps

you never do

–

His voice dies away

Then he takes in the sight
of young people
smoking outside the window

in short skirts

–

Even though it's winter

–

I notice that the watch
I brought for him

–

The men's watch
with a wide leather strap
and tin embroidery

which I found
in Mama's dresser

–

He's not
wearing it

–

He'd rolled
up his sleeves
baring it all

–

Every wound he
made where the veins
whirl on

–

And before I
have a chance to
comment on them

he says:

–

Sandra

You can see
that I'm not entirely
comfortable
right

and I lean
forward

–

Caress
one streak of wound
which is deep red

and surprisingly dry

–

That felt nice
he says and
smiles at me

that's when I
start crying

–

And when I get home
I pick up my telephone and
write to him

that I should have
said something

–

I was just about
to say something

About those wounds
on your arms

–

I wouldn't be able
to see something like that
I wrote

and not care

–

And he replied

I know

IX

(PER)

My child
thrust forth like
bedrock

alive without
a name

–

So they place
her in my arms
give her to me
to hold

–

And the ocean
keeps pushing
us together

washing me up
from its depths

–

with this roar and
compulsion to be

–

Sit still now
don't go

–

Just bear it

keep holding on

–

Grow into
the wisdom

that this child
radiates

–

Dear Manal

–

How are we to keep
our promise

–

We are hopeless

unfit in every way

–

Half-Swedes who
laze about at home

\-

Eyes so dark
they seemed
barely there

as you walked proud
with your belly

\-

But here I can
breathe now

with the child
in my arms

\-

As if behind a
calm stone

You are rolled away

\-

We're just going
to stitch her up a bit
says the midwife

Don't worry

\-

Little do they know
Manal

\-

the ways in which
you've gone to pieces

–

Why didn't we
break up

the psychologist
had wondered
we were still so
young after all

–

And your mother
who said:

You can't keep
going like this

–

A living child
a strong child

–

The smell of body
from your hair

The smell of
hot blood
the smell of sea
and salt

–

The smell of depth
from the gossamer leaf
of a sleeping face

–

I have a child

I keep time
alive in my
arms

–

Where shall we
take our bodies
Manal

–

Are we not
already home

X

Homegoing, Messaure. Guorbak, Porjus. 1999

(PER, SANDRA)

Each morning
I wake the hands
of thought

reaching for
their gentle tools

–

creating patterns
in the world

–

But the place where
work and love
flow into one

–

is so hard to find

–

Maybe home
has withered

where recently it had grown

–

The summer
I got my first job

It was like
following
the tides

–

I spent my evenings
running through
the forest

–

Sandra quipped
that a Lapp doesn't
run without
reason

–

doesn't go anywhere
without errand

–

In the mornings
I was drawn deep
into the mountain

I held my breath

–

Went around with
my binder in hand
stood aside and
made an effort

read off lists

—

By lunch
I was already finished
with my rounds

still I lingered

—

Leafing through
the binder

walking back
and forth studying
the circuit diagram cards

—

Anything to avoid
taking a seat
with the others

pretending to drink
my coffee

—

Laughing out loud and
just enough

nodding along
with a smile

During their hours-long
discussions
about faulty
power plants

—

and Vattenfall's
politics

—

One morning I heard
steps across the floor

—

It was a half-boss
I barely knew
the name of

I had never
learned his name

—

Even though he'd
been above me
all this time

—

I can't explain it
but I hear
myself say:

–

For me it's pretty slow
here in the daytime

–

Can't I start coming
in at night instead

I'd be able to finish
my tasks in a few
hours at night

–

If only I had
some peace and quiet

I could be
at home during the day
doing other things

–

Then he asks me
aren't you
Rolf's boy

–

But I say no

I say nothing more

–

I spent my nights
running

–

Music from a
wedding reception

spilled from
the hotel

–

Mama said

that there was a
portrait of my ex-
girlfriend's
grandfather
in there

in the restaurant

–

That there was
an artist from elsewhere
who'd come to paint
the folks from here

–

Her grandfather
was among them

–

one of those
German soldiers'
bastard sons

–

Manal has never
even been down
in the power plant

–

She's never seen
the huge mosaic about
the construction of
hydroelectric power

with old Sámi gods
all around

–

But I have
That time

–

when I tried
to work with the river

–

That time

Per was in the hands of
the streams

–

I let Andreas
take me to his
roaring ocean
of reindeer

let their waves
drown me out

–

They ran in
circles in the
round enclosure
scattering
my thoughts

grunting

–

their hoofs clicking

–

Andreas in
the waves

–

He caught
the calf and pulled
it to him

marked its ear

–

Strands of fur sticking
to the hot blood

on his
bare fingers

–

Then his dad
talked to me

almost warily
about the fells

–

Recalling the fires
that he and his parents have
lit upon each slope

–

He said that Andreas
would live with the reindeer
like they do

–

Like he's done since
he was a boy

it was the whole point

–

His son

carrying on his
forefathers' legacy

–

To me it sounds a bit
overblown

–

The rain drummed
stubbornly on
the tent's tarp

–

We boiled coffee

watched the smoke rise

–

A baby cousin
walked alone singing close
to the tent where Andreas
and I were resting

Another came
in to say hello

–

Andreas stretched
out on his side
and scratched his
father's dog

–

It was called Rádná

He said that all
their dogs had
been called Rádná

–

When the first one
died he'd wanted
to bury it

But there was frost
in the ground so he
had to put it in the freezer
chest until the earth
thawed

–

As the fire
moved to die
he whispered softly

–

Tell me
what it was like
for you

the first time

–

And I told him

–

but about a
different time

I got into
a car with my friend

–

There were two older
boys sitting
in the front

A barbell was waiting
silvery and large
in its black rack

at the back of the
apartment

–

For a pair of sweaty
fists

–

We kissed

and those fists were
set on enticing
pleading and nagging

–

Still I said no

I didn't want to

374

–

Like you didn't
want to give me
your number Andreas said
laughing

–

I could hear
my heart racing

–

fast as
young foxes

my cheeks turned red
and the night
gleamed

–

That time

by the ocean
of reindeer

–

Three times
Andreas and I had
crossed swords
already

–

At those Sámi debates

where his words
made me scream:

–

How can you not
have noticed

–

That the Sámi who are
not reindeer herders
are forced out of the
picture of our people

never to be let
in again

–

After the Swedes
arrived and drew
their borders

–

Said that the one
is a Lapp and the
other not

–

I cried out to him

That this is how to
break a people

–

But he just
sat there fermenting

in the packed
movie theater

–

So sure of everything
to do with his Sámi language
and his reindeer
earmark

–

He laughed at me

said that I was dippy

–

That the reindeer
herding issues were
the only true issues

the only way

–

to take back control
of the land

–

He said that the rest
is just emotion

–

Later

I came home
to my own bed

—

I closed my eyes

tried to picture a
home and a life

—

Thought that surely

—

Andreas wouldn't become
one of those men
like my papa

—

Who when he couldn't
bring himself to leave
a crying child at day care

he took me to my mother
at her workplace

—

tried to leave me
with her instead

–

That time

when I was a girl
at my father's side

XI

Padjelanta. Summer 1995

(PER)

I ride the
tourist boat
in the sun

–

Then walk for hours
in hot boots

squinting

–

It's as if night
will never come

the fells
keep brightening
around me

–

Finally I see
at the farthest end

of the fell heath
the spread of lake

–

I sink down

on one of the gray rocks
only noticing now
that I am freezing cold

–

The lake water shuts
blindly

dark around the rocks
I'm throwing

–

Hey you

a voice says

–

Aren't you Lise's boy

–

And I notice
down by the water
obscured by
the bushes

–

is a person in a
rowboat

–

What are you
doing up here
he asks

–

He explains that
he has been sitting
there waiting

for someone
to come
this way

–

Someone usually
always comes
sooner or later

he says with
a smile

–

He was thinking of rowing
to the other side

Because he had a
cloudberry patch there

–

He asks
me if I need
a ride across the lake

—

After we've talked
awhile

I realize that
this is old man
Koljok

—

As soon as he starts to row
water streams
into the boat

—

You've got a scoop there
he says

and nods at my feet

—

I start bailing

Koljok rows along

—

The lake drives waves
this way and that
he sets aside
his oars for a bit

—

And takes out a
pair of thin gloves
from the pocket of his
anorak

Then he rows on

–

I warm up fast

Way over there
I see the barren
rocky shore

–

So what'll you be
up to after the summer
he asks and drops
the oars back into the boat

are you in school

–

I keep bailing
and reply that no
I've graduated

And I have asthma
so I got out of military service

–

That's the thing I guess
I say

I don't really
know what
to do

–

Won't Vattenfall
take care of that
he says

You end up there
the lot of you one by one

XII

The old Porjus power station. 1989

(SANDRA)

I stood there looking on
as my friend sold
Vattenfall's books

–

The lies burned
from the titles
in the tourist's hands

–

Now she was going to read

About its great exploit
in the backwoods
its pioneer power stations
in the wilderness

–

How long would they
keep getting away

–

With writing
our actions and
our grazing grounds

our entire cultural
landscape
out of history

–

By calling
everything wilderness
and backwoods

–

The power station
a castle in the midst
of the forest

They'd eagerly
cleared away the lichen
trampled on our language
upset our seite

–

Now I walk around here
guiding tourists

–

Showing and telling
until impressed they
point out the windows

as beautiful as
church windows

–

Right into the control
room I plan to climb as
soon as they go to lunch

and spray-paint all over
the white marble

–

Then I hear footsteps
in the corridor

A familiar whistling
sailing
through the air

–

And I see Papa

–

There he is in
the doorway asking:

Want to come with
me to the grill for a bite

XIII

In the car. Close to Porsi. Fall 1988

(SANDRA)

Like cool soft
hands the river ran
along the earth

–

Like silent soft
hands I watched it
run as if along

a face

–

Mama sat still

with her eyes on the road

–

Her fingers came to
rest on the wheel

–

And she filled the whole
car with silence
and questions

but I sensed

–

That I should
let her be

–

I noticed she'd
grown a few coarse
gray strands
at her hairline

and a reindeer
sprang up

–

at the roadside

–

Waited calmly in the ditch

whiffed the wind

–

It's eerie actually
Mama said

I guess I wasn't
really listening

–

But she was saying that
the road was eerie
running like it did so
empty and long

–

She slowly started to
tell me about the time
she took her driving exam

–

The examiner wanted

them to drive
far down
the highway

–

They were
alone in the car

–

Mama kept driving
miles upon miles

–

Open road
and forest as far
as the eye could see

not a person
not a house

–

And then between
Porjus and Gällivare
she said

the examiner puts his hand
on my crotch

–

So I say to him

If you're going to do that
I won't be able to concentrate
on my driving

–

And I laughed
with Mama who
was also laughing

–

One time
she continued

One time I took
the car

–

Rolf had been
called out in the night
it was probably the first
year we were together

The men were working
up in Ritsem

–

It was summer

and I couldn't
sleep because it was
unusually hot

–

I woke up early

–

Rolf wasn't back yet

And I had the idea
of taking the car to a small
lake up in the forest

where we'd gone swimming once

–

It was nice
up there
but full of midges
hot

–

I glided out into the water

and then lay down
to sunbathe

–

While I'm
lying there a man
turns up

I'm squinting into the sun
and can just about
see him

–

He's standing by
my head peering
down at me

–

I hear him
touching
himself

–

For a long time
he keeps going

I don't dare
move a muscle

–

I just lie there with
my eyes shut and
holding still

–

until he's done
then he leaves

–

Mama fell silent

and I sensed
the same silence
fall in me

–

In that moment we both saw

something out
on the road
right in front of the car

–

It was a reindeer carcass

–

I shouted: Watch out
and right as we
were braking to a stop

a great golden eagle
rose up
from the reindeer

–

Colossal

As wide as the car
from wingtip to
wingtip

–

I hadn't even
noticed it
was there

–

We sat in silence

watching the eagle fly

–

First it flew low

close to the asphalt

–

Then it rose and
rose until it was
out of view

And Mama said
that she wondered whose
reindeer this was

–

I'll have to call Erik Utsi
she said and started
the car

–

To tell him that there's
a dead reindeer

on the road

XIV

(SANDRA)

I yoik in the church

ascending in agility
expanding in
agility

–

Emotions'
clang
tongues

my emotions
are tongues
and eyes

–

Words from my
tongue rise higher
and higher up

through the
painted ceiling

–

Mama wipes away
tears with her shawl
friends clap

–

Later on the church hill
a hug from the priest

–

Sandra keep
up the yoiking
she says as we
walk across the gravel

–

Then she tells
us that she was
the first to yoik
in a Swedish church

Once it became legal

–

In the car Mama
holds her cigarette

out the window

–

I tell her about the
crafts teacher asking
if I might like to
sew myself a kolt

She'd promised to help me

–

Should the buttons
on the belt
be round or square
I ask eagerly

–

Or are square buttons
only for when
you're married

But Mama shakes
her head:

–

I don't know Sandra
I don't know those things

XV

Then we walked in silence
along the sea

Mama and I

–

With care
I tightened my shoes
around my feet

I could tell
the fasteners
were worn out

–

The water sparkled

and I took
off my sweater

–

Mama sat alone
on the dock

–

She was
thinking of that
boy's days

She was
wondering what Nila
had been doing here

–

I'm sure
she was

–

Papa had already
gone back with
Sandra

–

He was going to help
her ask
for the toilet

And I was thinking
about him driving
us here

–

I'd been sitting
with Mama in
the back seat

for long stretches
it was as quiet
as a closet

–

The sun bore down
on my video game
it dimmed

and I had to tilt
the screen up to
keep the light off

–

At the gas station Papa
parked with great care
he'd been at the wheel all
morning

–

He sat still
while Mama climbed
out of the car to refuel

–

I was too hot

There was a tired itch
in my glassy eyes
a creeping in my hair

–

The first hour

they'd talked
about things that happened
a long time ago

–

Maybe even before
they were born

–

Papa had enough

and shook his head

–

Ran his hand
through his hair
and stared

While Mama
kept talking fast
and at length

–

The road was long
gray out there

–

She said of course
no Sámi had
as hard a time as
people in other countries

–

Then she fell silent

and Papa stayed silent

–

And everything was as
usual but she
was sad

–

And the boy's
grave that she wanted
to look for

–

which might not
even exist

–

It had made
Papa sad

–

The sea was crashing
into the dock on which
Mama sat

–

It was rocking gently
this way and that and
all was silent

The world
stretched out
unknowing

—

I saw the mute pines
growing
beyond the reeds

I saw the blades of grass
and the closed
stones

—

All the white
hospital walls
I saw

—

All that

which would never
be able to speak
to my mother

—

Should we go back
I asked her

And said maybe
the graves were
nearer the woods

—

So there we were awhile

searching for
the grave site

–

My muddy shoes
pinching

My jeans straining
at the hip and
the bite on my arm
itching

–

The waves crashed

foamed and
turned

–

The shuttered hospital

the white buildings

–

Mama's eyes

searching
searching

–

And Papa's shouts
before he started
the car

—

I saw Mama point

—

And I looked
up at a great
black clock

high atop
the tower above
the entryway

—

Facing the sea

XVI

The apartment in Porjus. Pentecost 1984

(SANDRA)

Do you have to let
the heat out
Papa shouts

It's when Mama
vacuums that Papa has
to shout the loudest

–

Now he's leaving
the couch and closing
the window she
just opened

he hurries back
to Per with a
naughty grin

–

Well look what's still
knocking around
Mama shouts

–

And she shuts
off the vacuum cleaner
with her foot

bends down
in front of the bookshelf
and picks up one
of the vinyl records

–

And I give it a tug
because I want to
see

–

But she snatches
it away from me

–

Then it's funny

because the guy singing
has a squeaky voice

and all the girls
singing along are singing
even more squeakily

–

Mama sings along
and her singing
is better than theirs

And she can sing
in Sámi too which
I didn't know

–

Then Papa shouts:

Lise isn't this
where they sing

that every Sámi girl
is worth ten Swedish ones

XVII

Porjus churchyard. Fall 1983

(SANDRA)

We have shoveled earth
Mama with bare
hands of tears

–

I clung
to a rose

–

It pricked me
and bloodied
my white sleeve

like a coloring
from you Grandma

–

With your red cap
and those red shawls

–

Now we have buried you

and people turned up
who I'd never seen before

–

Many wore kolts
just like you
used to

–

Mama had given
me a red rose
to carry to the grave

–

But first they carried
the casket out of the church

–

Mama dropped
her red rose first
then me

–

The hardest part
was stepping right up
to the open grave

–

My legs were weak

I was afraid
of falling in

if I stood
close to its edge

–

There was a thud
from down below
where the rose landed
and broke

And then an old woman
came over and cried

–

She cried and called
to you Grandma

–

Then she fell to
her knees and cried
even more

until two younger folks
helped her up

–

The old woman was
wearing a blue kolt and
the younger two's were green

–

Mama's dress
was new and black

and the rest of us wore
regular clothes

–

And all around the
forest was yellow and red
because it's fall now
Grandma

–

Later when Papa
was standing with Per and
Uncle Jonne

–

up by
the rowans

–

I saw that Mama
was on her own

Everyone else
had gone away
from the grave

–

But Mama had stayed

So I had to
go to her and
keep her company

−

That's enough waiting

the woman down there
has been scattered
with the sea

−

Its waves have
already steeped
her thoughts

that ray has
faded out

−

Scrape up some earth
from your homeland and
keep it in your jacket
pockets

−

She will never be
recovered in the sand

−

But she has
been home and
not home

she has been
where her
memories were

–

They were never
in rooms or walls
but in person

in the living and dead
and in the words
with which she moved

–

Next time Grandma

I intend to wear
my kolt like you

XVIII

After the funeral

(A PRIEST)

Autumn came

it soared up
over the dam
the river valley

–

It sank
over the earth

–

Once
there were many
children here

and their cheeks
were ruddied
with play

–

The new priest
stands beneath
the rowans

she was the one to bury
this woman

–

The funeral oration she'd held
still lingered
in her head

–

They had never
met in life

And she had
visited the family
at home

–

asked them to tell her
about the woman who
was now gone

–

She tucked the snus up
with her tongue
stayed put and
thought awhile

–

They had offered
so little when she'd said:

Can't you
tell me
about her life

what she was like

–

Down in the parish yard

the caretaker set
out the new chairs

–

The two children's
parents hugged
the crying girl
for a long time

then left
the grave

–

The young boy
ran through

the autumn leaves
fell all over

–

A quiet rain

Landed on the rocks
and the dry
grass

sailed over the hill
where she stood

–

She watched how the family
she didn't know well
but still had gotten to follow
quite closely for a while

How they went away
how they slowly
disappeared

–

down the freshly raked
gravel paths

–

And she wondered
who they were

NOTE

In Northern Sámi, the word *Ædnan* means the land, the earth, and my mother. It sounds similar to the word *ædno*, "the river," and *ædni*, "the mother." In today's orthography these words are written as *eana(n)*, *eatnu*, and *eadni*. Etymologically they seem to come from the same root word, which roughly means "great."

ACKNOWLEDGMENTS

The author most gratefully acknowledges the generous support and encouragement of Daniel Sandström, John Freeman, Johanna Lindborg, Saskia Vogel, and Daniel Pedersen.

Together with the translator, the author would like to thank Princeton University, and its Translator in Residence program and Native American and Indigenous Studies Initiative, for their invaluable support in the completion of this translation.

A NOTE ABOUT THE AUTHOR

Linnea Axelsson is a Sámi-Swedish writer, born in the province of North Bothnia in Sweden. In 2018, she was awarded the August Prize for this book. She lives in Stockholm, Sweden.

A NOTE ON THE TYPE

This book was set in Sabon, a typeface designed by the well-known German typographer Jan Tschichold (1902–74). Sabon's design is based upon the original letter forms of the sixteenth-century French type designer Claude Garamond and was created specifically to be used for three sources: foundry type for hand composition, Linotype, and Monotype. Tschichold named his typeface for the famous Frankfurt typefounder Jacques Sabon (c. 1520–80).

Composed by North Market Street Graphics
Lancaster, Pennsylvania

Printed and bound by Friesens
Altona, Manitoba

Designed by Jo Anne Metsch